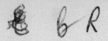

"Would you call me a coward?"

"Never in a hundred years, Joe."

The air crackled around them. Dixie knew it was a mistake to be alone, had known the tension would be unbearable. Add to that the fact that she had to touch him, to run her fingers through his hair, which brought back a thousand memories....

"Let's just get it over with."

He flinched with every cut. So did she. Nerves, she told herself. It was a lot of pressure cutting his hair.

Liar.

She took up the scissors again and worked methodically, her nerves sizzling, hands shaking.

He pointedly looked at them, then at her face.

"Harder than I thought," she said.

"For me, too." He took her hands in his, the point of the scissors dangerously closer to his heart. "But not just because of my hair."

Dear Reader,

My parents were childhood sweethearts. They met at 12, married at 20, and would've celebrated their 50th anniversary had they not died a couple of years before that auspicious event, only two months apart. Theirs was a love story for the ages.

Joseph McCoy and Dixie Callahan are childhood sweethearts, too, with a love story for the *pages,* as I've started calling it. Like many a long-term relationship, theirs hits a bump in the road, requiring a second look at who they are and where they should go next. It's a story about identifying and encouraging individual needs in order to make a stronger union.

I hope you enjoy the journey Joe and Dixie take to get there.

Susan

AT LONG LAST,
A BRIDE

SUSAN CROSBY

Silhouette

SPECIAL EDITION®

Published by Silhouette Books

America's Publisher of Contemporary Romance

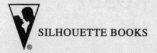

SILHOUETTE BOOKS

PLEASE RECYCLE
THIS PRODUCT IS RECYCLABLE

ISBN-13: 978-0-373-65525-0

Recycling programs
for this product may
not exist in your area.

AT LONG LAST, A BRIDE

Visit Silhouette Books at www.eHarlequin.com

Printed in U.S.A.

Books by Susan Crosby

Silhouette Special Edition

*The Bachelor's Stand-In Wife #1912
**The Rancher's Surprise Marriage #1922
*The Single Dad's Virgin Wife #1930
*The Millionaire's Christmas Wife #1936
††The Pregnant Bride Wore White #1995
††Love and the Single Dad #2019
‡The Doctor's Pregnant Bride? #2030
††At Long Last, a Bride #2043

Silhouette Desire

†Christmas Bonus, Strings Attached #1554
†Private Indiscretions #1570
†Hot Contact #1590
†Rules of Attraction #1647
†Heart of the Raven #1653
†Secrets of Paternity #1659
The Forbidden Twin #1717
Forced to the Altar #1733
Bound by the Baby #1797

*Wives for Hire
††The McCoys of Chance City
†Behind Closed Doors
**Back in Business
‡The Baby Chase

SUSAN CROSBY

believes in the value of setting goals, but also in the magic of making wishes, which often do come true—as long as she works hard enough. Along life's journey she's done a lot of the usual things—married, had children, attended college a little later than the average coed and earned a B.A. in English. Then she dove off the deep end into a full-time writing career, a wish come true.

Susan enjoys writing about people who take a chance on love, sometimes against all odds. She loves warm, strong heroes and good-hearted, self-reliant heroines, and she will always believe in happily ever after.

More can be learned about her at www.susancrosby.com.

For Mom and Dad,
and for childhood sweethearts everywhere.

Chapter One

"I'm going to see Joe," Dixie Callahan announced to the woman standing at the bottom of the staircase watching her. Maebelle "Nana Mae" McCoy was leaning on her purple cane, studying Dixie's face. Dixie hoped she didn't look like she was about to face a firing squad, although she felt like it.

"I'm glad you finally called him. It's time." Nana Mae waved an arthritic finger at Dixie. "I saw it coming yesterday at the wedding, you know. My grandson couldn't take his eyes off you."

Ah, yes. The wedding—Dixie's fifth trip down the aisle in two years. At age thirty, she'd become a living cliché: always a bridesmaid, never a bride. The wedding had brought home how she should've been married long ago—to Joe. She'd barely slept last night thinking about it.

"*He* called *me*," Dixie admitted, correcting Nana Mae's misperception, wondering how much more she should say. Even though she felt closer to Joe's grandmother than her own, confiding about her grandson was tricky. "I don't know what he wants," Dixie said finally, settling for a simple truth.

Like Nana Mae, Dixie had also caught him eyeing her a lot at his brother's wedding yesterday. Had he realized then, as she had, that it was a year to the day since they'd broken up? A year usually marked an end to a mourning period. And she'd mourned plenty.

"No matter what happens today, it *is* time, Dixie," Nana Mae said gently, patting her cheek.

"I know. I'll see you later."

She left Nana Mae's cozy house, Dixie's home for the past six months, got into her car and let it warm up, her thoughts on what was ahead, possibilities bombarding her. Hope also seeped in, against her efforts to block it. Had the wedding made him reconsider? Did he want to try again? Set a date this time?

With the car heater blasting, she backed out of the driveway. Any other time, she would've enjoyed the crisp mid-November day. The small Sierra foothills community of Chance City, California, smelled of fireplace smoke and fallen leaves damp from an overnight rain. A few hardy leaves still clung to branches, specks of gold and brown against the gray sky.

Dixie barely acknowledged the scenery, except to consider how her curly blond hair would be uncontrollably curlier in the humid air, just when she wanted to look her best.

Her heart thundered as she drove the three blocks to Joe's house. In the driveway sat his new pickup, Four Seasons Lawn and Landscaping painted neatly on the doors, mobile advertising for the business he'd started when they were both sixteen. What had begun as a one-man, one-mower operation had grown into a thriving enterprise with twenty employees.

She'd heard that he'd been branching out this past year, too, his dedication to eco-friendly landscaping techniques garnering attention outside of their small community, enough that he'd created a second company, LandKind. His drive and business sense had taken him far.

Dixie didn't park in the driveway next to his truck, her spot for the eight years they'd lived together, but on the street. As she walked toward the house, she realized she should have met him somewhere else, or even have come on foot, so that she might slip inside the house with less chance of anyone seeing her. Instead, her parked car was like a neon sign announcing she was here. One phone call from a neighbor to a McCoy would set the rumor mill in motion.

"Too late now," she muttered. Hearing the distinctive sound of leaves being raked, she made her way to the backyard. The space was awash in yellow, orange and white—mums, marigolds and nasturtiums, and other flowers she couldn't name.

He apparently couldn't hear her approach over the sound of his raking, even though she didn't tiptoe. In the forty-degree weather he wore a long-sleeved T-shirt bearing his company logo, jeans and boots, his compact body solid. His long brown hair was secured away from his face, as clean shaven as always.

Joseph McCoy was as much a temptation to her now as he'd been when they were teenagers. She had no illusions about that ever changing.

She stuffed her hands into her jacket pockets. "Hi," she said.

He spun around. "Dix. Thanks for coming."

She couldn't read his expression. For most of her life she'd been able to read him.

Because he let you.

True. Now he didn't.

"Let's go inside," he said, leaning the rake against a rock wall he'd built the first week they'd moved in.

They headed to the back door, which led into the kitchen. She followed him through it, then the dining room, ending up in the living room, where embers glowed in the stone fireplace. She didn't look around, not wanting to see if he'd changed anything. They'd remodeled the entire house and yard—together.

"Can I take your coat?" he asked.

"I'm okay." She wrapped it tighter around her and sat in a rocking chair that had belonged to her great-grandmother. When Dixie had left Joe, she'd taken only her clothes with her, leaving behind material goods and shared memories, and those tumbled through her mind now as she watched him hunker at the fireplace, adding tinder, then some small logs.

"So, what's up?" she asked, linking her fingers.

"You know what yesterday was."

"Your brother Donovan's wedding," she said lightly, wanting him to just say it, whatever *it* was. He'd called her, after all. It was his show to run.

"A year ago yesterday you returned my engagement ring." He set the fireplace screen in place then sat across from her, making and keeping eye contact.

It was as if he was blaming her, when he was the one at fault. "After fifteen years of being together, you wouldn't set a date," she reminded him.

He nodded, took a moment, then said, "It's time, Dix." His words echoed Nana Mae's.

Hope leaped in her heart. He'd seen the error of his ways? No. His expression wasn't full of love. "Time for what?" she asked, but already knowing the answer.

"To move on." He leaned his elbows on his knees. "Everyone keeps waiting for something to happen between us. We need to finish it."

She thought she'd been prepared for the words. Still, it shocked her to the core.

She also knew he was right, but it was so hard to admit it. After being Joe-and-Dixie for sixteen years— even this last year when they hadn't been together—

they wouldn't be two halves of a whole anymore, but individuals.

"What do you want me to do? Make some kind of announcement?" she asked. "Does it need to be official in order for everyone to stop expecting us to get back together?" *Including me?* She hadn't really realized how much she'd still been hoping, not until this moment.

And suddenly she knew what he would say next....

"I think we should sell the house, Dix. Or one of us buy the other out."

Joe said the words quickly, needing to get them out. He wished there was some other way to tell her, didn't want to see her expression, her hurt.

"Your timing couldn't be more perfect," she said firmly, setting her hands on her thighs. "Let's do it." She stood, headed for the door.

"Do you want to buy my share?" he asked as she pulled open the door.

"No. I need the money." She turned her head slightly, not looking at him. "Are you going to leave town?"

"It's my turn."

She nodded in understanding. "What about your business here?"

"I'm learning to delegate."

"Good for you. Well, let me know what I can do," she said, then she was gone, her strides long and purposeful.

He stared after her, caught off guard at the speed of her exit.

"I'm doing this for you, Dix," he said into thin air as

her car pulled away. She hadn't let him explain why. And what did she mean by the timing being perfect? He hadn't heard any rumors about her, not that she was leaving town or renting a place of her own, rather than helping out Nana Mae in exchange for room and board.

He finally had a chance to do what he'd wanted forever—to broaden his world. He was in big demand all over the western states, could very well be gone for months at a time. Dixie never dreamed of traveling, was always content to be home. It was where she belonged, whereas he'd known his roots weren't as firmly planted, for all that he loved his family and work and town. He'd had his own dreams, and he finally had a chance to fulfill them, just like his brothers had. Now they were back home—and it was his turn.

And part of his moving on was setting her free, too, because even though they hadn't been together for a year, neither of them had made significant changes. Hadn't started dating. Someone had to end that stalemate, even if technically she had by throwing his ring in his face.

They'd both lived in limbo ever since, given their history of breaking up and reconciling a few times through the years.

He stared into space. He should be happy. He'd gotten what he wanted—her agreement that they should sell the house. Why didn't that make him happy?

Because once again he'd hurt her. Even though she'd tried to hide it, she had not been prepared for his news. It didn't matter that he'd endured a lot of long, lonely, painful hours, too. He didn't want Dixie to be hurt anymore.

Joe looked at his watch, grateful he had a reason to get out of the house. He'd be a little early for his appointment, but it was better than staying here, where he could still smell her perfume.

He drove to the heart of town, to the Take a Lode Off Diner, which would be packed for brunch with the after-church crowd.

When he stepped into the noisy restaurant, a silence gradually came over the place, leaving it quiet enough to hear competing songs from the individual jukeboxes in the red leatherette booths. Every customer's gaze fixed on him.

Well. That didn't take long. Obviously, word had spread that Dixie was at the house this morning.

"Hey, Joe!" called the Lode's owner, Honey, as she came out from behind the counter, a plate in each hand, her long, gray braid swinging. "Lemon meringue pie just came out."

"I'll take a slice, thanks, after lunch. You know what I want."

Conversation picked up again as he made his way to the last booth, where the man he'd asked to meet him sat, drinking coffee. Everyone either grinned or winked at Joe. He ran a hand down his face, then addressed the crowd. "Dixie and I are not getting back together, so whoever called you or you called, please set them straight."

Cell phones came out almost as one. He laughed—

how could he not?—and was still laughing when he reached the man he'd come to see, who also apparently had nothing better to do, since he'd arrived early, too.

"How's it going?" Joe asked, addressing Landon Kincaid, whom everyone called by his last name. He'd graduated from high school only a few years before Joe, but they'd never been close friends.

"Everything's great, thanks," Kincaid said after shaking hands. "You've got me curious, though."

"Did you already order lunch?"

"Yeah. What's going on, Joe?"

"Dixie and I want to put our house on the market."

Kincaid's brows went up. "Now?"

"Now."

"Your chances are better in the spring."

"Can't wait. Thanks," Joe said to Honey as she poured him a mug of coffee.

She started to leave, then touched his shoulder. "We were only *hoping* for a reconciliation, you understand. It wasn't malicious."

"I get it. It's Chance City. It's okay."

A few seconds passed, then Kincaid said, "Why me? There are plenty of Realtors around. My guess is one of your enormous extended family works as one."

"Actually, no. Seems like we've got every other trade covered but that. Look, I know selling houses is the least of what you do, but I was hoping you'd handle this one. Have you got the time?"

"Sure. Winter's coming up. Everything slows down."

He sipped his coffee. "I haven't been inside your house, but I know you've invested a lot of sweat equity in it."

Labors of love. "I think you'll find it turnkey for a new buyer. I don't expect to be in town very much in the near future, so you'll probably have to work with Dixie on this most of the time."

"My pleasure."

A memory flashed then of Kincaid and Dixie dancing at the wedding reception yesterday, more than once. They'd talked the whole time, mostly looking serious. But then, Kincaid generally seemed serious. When he wasn't being a Realtor, he scooped up properties and renovated them, sometimes reselling, sometimes renting. He was driven and motivated—and a mystery ever since he'd moved to town, alone, as a high school junior. Legally emancipated, he'd lived by himself and worked as much as the law allowed. Now he owned half of Chance City—or so it seemed.

Honey delivered their meals. By the time they were eating dessert, they had a plan for the sale and a gentleman's agreement, paperwork to follow.

Joe's cell phone rang as he finished eating. "Hey, Mom."

"I need a favor. You know we're throwing a dinner for the out-of-town wedding guests. Ethan's in need of some attention while we put the meal together. Poor kid. He's surrounded by women."

"Give him ten years and he won't complain about that. I'll be right there."

Kincaid's phone had rung, as well. "I'll be right there," he said, at the same time as Joe, then smiled when Joe laughed. "Business to tend to," Kincaid said.

"A five-year-old nephew to rescue," Joe said, pulling out his wallet. He grabbed Kincaid's check, as well as his own, dropped a few bills on the table. "I'll get this. Thanks for taking time out of your Sunday."

Kincaid nodded. "I'll have the appraiser out sometime tomorrow, if that works for you."

Joe held up his cell phone. "You know how to find me."

They walked out of the diner together, but headed in opposite directions. Joe climbed into his truck just as Kincaid reached his silver SUV. He didn't get in but continued on up the street, lifting a hand now and then to people driving by. Even though he kept to himself mostly, he was well liked. Or at least, Joe had never heard any rumors about the man….

Including about women.

He wasn't a player. Stable. Beyond comfortable financially. Steady. Committed to Chance City.

Like Dixie.

Joe shifted in his seat. His breath went shallow. If he could find someone to watch over Dixie, the kind of man she deserved, Joe could leave in peace. She'd given up all those years waiting for him. This could be his gift to her.

He could put them together, Kincaid and Dixie. He could make sure that she was the one to handle the sale of the house, force them to communicate, spend time together.

Kincaid had said, "My pleasure," when Joe had mentioned he would be gone a lot, leaving Kincaid to work with Dixie on the sale.

Hell, who wouldn't want her? She wanted what Joe couldn't give her, not for a long time to come—marriage and babies. He had to do the right thing and let her be with someone who could. He would get it all set up before he left town. Kincaid would be a good choice, Joe thought.

Even if it killed *him*.

Chapter Two

Dixie looked at herself in the mirror at the beauty shop where she worked, where she'd gone to hide. Her eyes looked hollow. She'd stopped herself from crying several times since she'd walked out on Joe an hour ago, midconversation. She knew he'd had more to say, but she couldn't stand there a second longer.

He'd decided to end their relationship with a final blow—selling their house.

She'd gotten in her car and left with no direction in mind. She couldn't go back to Nana Mae's. She couldn't go to her home away from home, Aggie McCoy's. Dixie couldn't involve Joe's mother in this, or any of the other

McCoys, who were closer to her than her own family, even her parents.

She'd had no place to go to but here, Bitty's Beauty Shoppe, where she'd worked since graduating from cosmetology school a few months ago.

Her future now. Her whole future, apparently.

Even with her heart breaking she understood Joe's need to go places and do things. All his adult life, after his father died when Joe was barely out of high school, he'd been taking care of everyone. Because his brothers were off creating exciting careers for themselves, Joe had taken it upon himself to watch over his five older sisters, his mother and grandmother. But now his brothers lived in Chance City again. His sisters were all married and settled.

As Joe had said, it was his turn.

Someone tapped on the front window. Kincaid smiled through the glass at her, then, as the owner of the building used his key to unlock the door and come inside. He'd been her first client when she'd started working at Bitty's, had immediately established a standing 9:30 a.m. appointment every third Friday.

"You're fast," she said. She'd called him barely ten minutes ago.

"I was in the neighborhood." He came toward her.

She extended a hand, preventing a hug, if that was what he'd intended. She felt raw and exposed, and didn't want anyone close, especially the megabusinessman Kincaid.

He eyed her closely, kindly, as if he could see her broken heart. It unnerved her a little.

"I take it you've made a decision," he said.

"Yes." She drew a shaky breath. "I want to do it. I want to buy the shop, rent the apartment upstairs. All of it."

"Congratulations."

"I said I *want* to. I'm not sure how I'm going to swing it financially, but I'll get it figured out. Bitty will work with me on it, I'm sure. She's anxious to move to Seattle before Christmas, in time for her first grandchild to be born. Maybe if I can give her enough down payment, she'll carry the loan."

Dixie looked around, picturing the changes she would make. She knew exactly what she wanted, had already gotten estimates for the work to be done. "She's not asking much, actually. It's like starting from scratch, since Bitty and I have been the only beauticians since Carole Ann left. The biggest expense will be the renovation. I plan to turn it into a day spa. I want this place to be a destination, so aside from lining up a couple more beauticians, I'll have to bring in a massage therapist; manicurist and an esthetician, build more rooms that are private and luxurious. I'm going to check with some bed-and-breakfasts and work out getaway-weekend deals with my spa."

"You've thought this through." He sat in one of the chairs as she wandered.

In her mind's eye she saw it finished, could even hear music playing, and voices, talking and laughing.

"I've been thinking about it for years, actually," she said. "It's timing, you know. Bitty decides to sell. The shop next door shuts down, so I can expand into that space. Luck was on my side."

"Oprah says luck is preparation meeting opportunity. I like that. It applies to me, too," Kincaid said.

"I hadn't looked at it that way, but it's true. I may be new to the salon business, but I managed my parents' hardware store for years, so I understand how business works, especially customer-service-oriented ones." She crossed her arms, looking around the room. "I've studied this particular business upside down and backward. I know what to do and how to do it. I surveyed my clients. I visited a whole bunch of spas so that I know what works, and what doesn't, and how to adapt for this particular location." She stopped her rapid-fire monologue and took a breath. "I just need someone to believe in me as much as I believe in myself. I want a chance to prove myself."

"I'll give you that chance, Dixie. I'll act as your banker."

Stunned, she struggled to find words. "I couldn't poss—"

"I do it all the time. The Bank of Kincaid, not open to the public, but loans available at reasonable rates."

Surprise lodged in her throat. "Um. That's a generous offer, thank you. But I want to establish my own credit, you know? Part of being a responsible businesswoman."

"I understand that, and I admire you for it. But if the bank turns you down, remember I'm your backup. Frankly, the amount you need is small potatoes. One way or the other you'll own this business."

"Why would you do that?"

"I think you're a low risk for default," he said. "You have skill and passion. People with a passion have a much better chance of succeeding."

Something bothered her about him. He said the right things, so it wasn't that. It was the way he looked at her, she decided. As if he knew something she didn't.

He stood then. "Full disclosure here, Dixie, before we go any further. Joe just asked me to be the listing Realtor on your house. I agreed."

She was taken aback by how fast Joe had set the process in motion. And he hadn't bothered to consult her on which Realtor to use—

"You don't approve?" Kincaid asked.

"No. I mean, yes. It's fine, I guess."

"I advised him it wasn't a good time to try to sell. Market's flat. We're headed into winter. He said he didn't want to wait. Is that how you feel, too?"

"My nest egg isn't very big. I could use the money from the sale. Even though my appointment book has been almost full since I started here, there are dry spells in any enterprise. I'll need a security net beyond the loan."

"If I may offer some advice?"

"Sure."

"The bank will want collateral, secured by your assets. Joe would have to be involved, because until it sells, your house is your collateral, and he owns half. After it sells, your cash will be your security on the loan, and made part of your contract. But until then, he's part of the deal. Do you think that will be a problem?"

"I doubt it, but I won't know without asking." After a year of avoiding each other, they were now being thrust together in order to end things. The irony didn't escape her.

"Show me some numbers, Dixie. Tell me what Bitty wants, what it'll take for the renovations. I can better advise you."

They spent the next half hour going over figures and estimating future costs, something that hadn't yet occurred to her, as she hadn't made her decision until today.

"When do you think you'll be open for business?" he asked, putting aside the pad of paper with numbers written all over it.

"I figure we'll be completely ready to go in three months. A Valentine's weekend opening," she said. "I've found a motor home to rent that's been set up as a mobile salon. I'll park it in the back lot. But I'll have the main room done first so that I can take the business indoors as soon as possible. Clients will be willing to put up with that temporary situation for only so long."

He shook his head. "I think you're being overly optimistic about the timing. Renovations could take up to twice that long, probably, speaking from experience."

"Two months to move back inside," she repeated. "Three months to completion."

"Care to make a friendly wager on that?"

She saw a glimmer in his eyes. "Sure. What's the prize?"

"For me, free haircuts for a year. You?"

"You pay for the new sign out front."

"Deal." They shook hands. "When will you be moving into the upstairs apartment?"

She stuffed her fists into her pockets. "I want to paint first, add my own colors, plus I have to get someone to replace me at Nana Mae's house. I won't leave until I know she'll be taken care of."

His sharp blue gaze pierced her. "Why haven't you asked me to do the remodel, Dixie? You know I've fixed up a lot of houses and several businesses."

"I need to handle it on my own." Everyone saw her as independent minded, but it wasn't the same as being a self-sufficient woman. She hadn't done much on her own before. Never lived alone. Never owned a business. She had a lot to prove, at least to herself. She'd always been proud—and a little envious—of how Joe had built a business from nothing. She would be starting with something already in place but turning it into something different—and hers.

"I understand that need," Kincaid said, giving her arm a slight squeeze. "Keep me in the loop, please, about the shop and your house."

After he left, she unlocked the door to the upstairs apartment, which had been without a tenant for a few months. Someday maybe she could buy a house of her own and expand the business into the upstairs. Or perhaps create a different business there.

Excitement and anxiety merged as she looked around

the space. Kincaid had updated the apartment a couple of years back, so the kitchen and bathroom were contemporary and clean. He'd replaced the windows with dual panes, keeping the Main Street noise to a minimum, and offering a good view of Chance City's downtown. Bundled in warm jackets, tourists wandered along the wood-plank walkways, enjoying the mother lode town and its gold-rush-era history. "Quaint," people called it.

Dixie had lived here her whole life, so it was just home to her. And this apartment? She might be a country girl at heart, but she was a romantic, too. She would give it a feminine touch, not having to please anyone but herself. She'd found a white eyelet bedspread at the consignment shop yesterday and snatched it up. She would design her space around it.

She would put her stamp on the salon, too, make it her own. Make it work.

After that, she would get serious about finding someone to love, to marry and have babies with. She'd waited a long time for that already, had always believed the man by her side would be Joseph McCoy. Their mostly on, occasionally off relationship had lasted sixteen years. Now it was over. No more making up.

Dixie relaxed her shoulders and rolled her neck, releasing the remaining tension. She felt good. Better than that—great. She was embarking on a new adventure into risky unknowns. Anticipation surged in her. She could be the Dixie she was before, but better. Stronger. More confident. Successful.

She would make her mark.

Dixie got in her car and headed for Sacramento, an hour's drive south, trusting the fact she would at least be able to move into the apartment, even if nothing else came through. Tomorrow was soon enough to deal with Joe and the loan.

Today she would escape and stay out of range, do a little shopping, because by the time she returned to Nana Mae's house tonight, the rumors would have spread, arousing if not satisfying curiosities.

But that was life in Chance City.

Chapter Three

Anticipation raced through Dixie early the next morning as she toweled off from her shower. She was excited and nervous at the same time. So much to do. First, she needed to talk to Joe. He'd left several messages yesterday on her cell phone that she'd decided to put off until today, but now was anxious to take care of.

She couldn't believe they were going to be tied together by the property, now that they'd decided to sell it. She hoped he would cooperate.

The dryer buzzed downstairs. Yanking on her robe, Dixie hurried to retrieve her clothes before the buzzer sounded again and woke up Nana Mae. At the bottom of the stairs she ran into Joe, literally. He grabbed her by the arms to stop her from knocking him down, then let go of her so fast she did almost fall.

Since she'd moved in six months ago, he'd stopped coming to visit his grandmother, even to do her yard, unless Dixie was gone.

"Why didn't you call me back?" he asked. "I—"

"Shh," she interrupted, taking him by the arm and pulling him into the kitchen, shutting the door. "Nana Mae is still asleep. Wait here."

She rushed into the laundry room, set the dryer on the cool-tumble cycle and turned off the buzzer, which she'd forgotten to do earlier.

Joe was filling his to-go cup with coffee when she returned, then he made himself at home at the kitchen table. "Do you have a minute?" he asked.

"Sure." She took a seat across the table, suddenly aware that she was naked under her robe, which was thick and fluffy, not showing anything that shouldn't be shown. But still, *she* knew she wore nothing underneath it. And he was wearing her favorite look—plaid shirt, down vest, jeans and boots. His cuffs were rolled up, exposing his forearms. She'd always loved his forearms.

Dixie squirmed a little in the chair as heat built inside her. Need. It'd been a whole year since he'd used those powerful arms to carry her to bed, something he'd done frequently….

"What's up?" she asked, her throat tight.

He frowned. "I needed to let you know that I talked to Kincaid about listing our house."

"I heard."

"You did? He called you?"

Implied in Joe's tone was, "You answered the phone for him but not me?"

"I called *him*," she said. "He's about to become my landlord. I'm buying the salon from Bitty, and I'm moving into the apartment upstairs."

Joe sat back. "Big changes for you."

"For sure. Did you ever picture me as a businesswoman?"

"I call what you did for your parents for all those years being a businesswoman. Don't you?"

"Yes. Thank you." She appreciated his recognition of her abilities. "But I'm facing some roadblocks, and I need your help to get over them."

"Whatever I can do, Dix. You know that."

"You may change your mind." She linked her fingers in her lap. "In order for me to get a loan for the purchase and remodeling, I need collateral. The only collateral I have is my share of the house. Which means you'll have to be involved, since you also own half. It's complicated."

Complicated because he would have some control over her future, and that was scary. She had to stay friendly with him, at a time when she also needed to keep away and let her heart heal.

"Actually, it's simple," he said. "You can count on me."

"I won't default on the loan."

"Of course you won't." He spun his coffee cup back and forth. "So, you'll be working with Kincaid?"

"To a point. He owns the building, not the business. But we spent time together, and he gave me good advice."

"Do you like him?"

Dixie cocked her head. What a strange question. What did it matter if she liked him or not? "I trust him, at least as far as business dealings are concerned. Why?"

"Because I expect you'll end up being the one to handle the house-sale business more than I will. It's good if you like him. Trust him."

"I do." She didn't tell him she'd been personally uncomfortable a couple of times, because she couldn't put her finger on why. Maybe she'd just been oversensitive, given how fresh her heartache was. But he'd seemed too interested—personally interested—and she wanted them to have a strictly business relationship. She got the sense he wanted more.

Which was perhaps why he'd been willing to lend her money. But did he want her beholden to him, or did it make good business sense? That was the question.

"But?" Joe asked, having waited through her silence.

"Oh. Nothing. Just normal fears about embarking on such an endeavor."

"When will you move out?"

"When I've lined up someone to take over here. I won't leave Nana Mae in the lurch."

"In what lurch?" the woman being discussed said as she swung the kitchen door open.

Joe popped up and led her to the table. She was a strong woman, a true matriarch, but Dixie always thought she looked fragile in the morning, before she was dressed for the day, before she applied a hint of blush and lipstick to brighten her face.

"I'm moving into my own place," Dixie said. "I've never lived alone. I need to."

Nana Mae nodded. "I agree, my dear."

Dixie put the teakettle on as grandmother and grandson talked, then she warmed the china teapot and a mug with hot water, filled an infuser with loose Earl Grey leaves. In a little while, she would fix oatmeal with dates and walnuts, and a poached egg. The breakfast menu rarely varied.

Dixie would miss her, this generous woman who had provided unconditional love and guidance. Tears burned Dixie's throat, welled in her eyes, made her heart ache. She kept her back to the others, poured the boiling water into the pot, then excused herself.

"I need to get dressed," she said, not looking at them. "Tea will be ready in a couple of minutes."

Dixie heard Joe drive off a little while later. She made her way downstairs.

"Joe left a key to the house for you," Nana Mae said, pushing it across the table toward Dixie.

"Thanks. Ready for breakfast?" she asked cheerfully while pocketing the key.

"If you are."

"I'm starving." Dixie moved around the kitchen, gathering what she needed. As soon as the oatmeal was cooking, she went into Nana Mae's bathroom and came back with her hairbrush, curling iron and hair spray. Sunlight poured onto the regal woman from the kitchen window as she sipped her tea, contentment on her face. Holding her mug in both hands to warm them, she closed her eyes.

"I'm going to miss this, Dixie. You've made my mornings such a pleasure."

Dixie didn't talk. She brushed the thinning silver hair over and over, then styled it into a youthful look just when it was time to ease the eggs into simmering water. She'd gotten the cooking-time process down to a science.

"You're too quiet," Nana Mae said when her food was set before her.

"Lots on my mind."

The older woman nodded. "I'm glad you and Joe have settled things."

"Me, too." Although it wasn't really, truly settled. It had taken them a year to get this far, after all. And they hadn't yet dated anyone in front of each other. That would be a major test.

"Here's some good news," Nana Mae said. "Our sweet Caroline was accepted at paramedic school. She was hinting that she wants to move in with me. So, it would seem there's no lurch to worry about."

Relief washed over Dixie. Joe's niece Caroline was twenty-five and responsible, not a party girl.

"As soon as possible," Nana Mae added.

Dixie smiled. "Are you kicking me out?"

"I'm giving you wings."

Dixie shoved away from the table to hug the woman who was so dear to her. "I'm so grateful for the time I lived with you. You are such an example to me in so many ways."

"I've loved having you. Maybe I could schedule a once-a-week appointment with you at the shop."

"Of course. Maybe for a massage and facial, too, now and then?"

Nana Mae blinked in surprise. "Well, why not?"

Dixie grinned. She felt secure enough that she would get a loan that she didn't mind word getting around, which it would now, with Nana Mae knowing. "I've got a lot to do today."

"Of course. Go, my dear. Enjoy this new stage of your life. I admire you, you know. You're very brave to do this on your own."

"I'm not on my own. So many people are support-ing me. How can I fail?" *Let me count the ways.* She ignored the skeptical little voice whispering in her head.

How could she feel so burdened yet so light at the same time? How could the air be so cold and her body so warm? How could she feel both happy and sad? Was this the new normal for her?

At least she was finally feeling something, after a year of tamping down her emotions. She could be ex-cited or scared or joyful or teary. It was all good.

Dixie was still smiling when she parked her car behind the beauty shop and walked to her parents' hardware store less than a block away. They opened at

7:00 a.m., ready to serve the tradesmen who also started early.

Her father, Malcolm, waved at her as he spoke to Maury the plumber. Dixie kept going to the rear of the store, where her mother, Beatrice, would be manning the parts department and the phone.

"Hey, Mom." Dixie swept the statuesque woman into a big hug. Although in her seventies, Bea was healthy and vital. It was her father Dixie worried about. He'd begun to show his age.

"I've been hearing rumors about you," Bea said.

"I'm the talk of the town these days." Dixie poured herself a mug of coffee, then dumped some powdered creamer in it. "No, Joe and I aren't getting back together. Yes, I'm buying Bitty's shop and turning it into a day spa. If you've heard anything else, tell me and I'll separate fact from fiction."

"That sets the record straight, I think." Bea angled around Dixie, looking for Malcolm. "Your father's a little hurt that you didn't buy the store. You've worked here since you were a kid. You know the business backward and forward. And we haven't had a single offer since we put it on the market after you quit."

"It's not my dream, Mom."

"Nor your brother's."

Dixie laughed. "Gavin's a doctor. You think he'd give that up?"

"He could buy it. Let someone else run it."

Dixie and her siblings were late-in-life babies, Gavin

having been born after their parents were married for almost twenty years, Dixie three years later, and their younger sister, Shana, two years after that. The siblings had been kept on tight leashes, not allowed the freedom that most children in the small community had, always having to account for their whereabouts. That hadn't stopped Shana from running away from home at eighteen and never returning.

Dixie had never forgiven her for that. She'd watched her parents suffer horribly at the loss of their daughter. Consequently, Dixie had felt obligated to fill in for her sister, too, being twice as much daughter.

"Someone will buy the store, Mom. And how is my big brother, the doctor?"

"He never writes. He never calls."

Dixie hadn't heard such bitterness from her mother before. She wasn't an overly positive kind of person, but not usually so negative, either. "What's going on, Mom?"

"I'm just tired. I'm seventy-one, you know, and I've been working here all my adult life. I want to rent an RV and travel before it's too late. And Dad's seventy-five. Who knows how much time he's got left."

"Why don't you promote Doug to manager? He's completely qualified, I think, after working here for fifteen years. He could hire someone to help temporarily. There are lots of qualified people looking for work during the off season, you know." It wasn't the first time Dixie had suggested the solution, but this time, she added something else. "I'll oversee the books, the bank deposits and the ordering. I know those are the things you worry about most."

"Are you serious?"

"Yes." Dixie stopped at that.

Bea hugged her, almost squeezing the breath out of her. "Thank you so much. You're a good daughter. I always knew you could be."

Now *there* was a backhanded compliment, as Nana Mae was fond of saying.

"Hey, sweetheart," her father said as he joined them.

"Hi, Dad." She gave him a hug, felt his bony ribs and wondered when he'd gotten so thin.

"Malcolm, guess what? Dixie's going to run the store for us so we can go away."

Her father turned a sharp gaze on her. "But I heard you were buying out Bitty."

"How did you hear that? I just decided yesterday."

"Bruno Manning was in this morning. Said he'd run some numbers for you on remodeling Bitty's shop. Was it a secret? If so, you should know that Bruno's got a big mouth."

"Thanks. I'll remember that. But Dad, I'm *not* going to run your store." She sent a that's-not-what-I-said glance at her mother, then repeated her offer to her father.

"Why would you do that?"

"Because I want you to enjoy yourselves. Get away. Have some fun. So go get yourself an RV. It's already late in the season to be taking off for parts unknown."

"Thank you." His voice shook.

Dixie didn't want to see him get emotional.

She was also biting off much more than she could chew by helping out her parents. She recognized that and would be prepared to hear about it from almost everyone in her life. However, it wouldn't be for too long. Her parents couldn't stay away for any length of time. But maybe they would start taking short trips more often, once they got a taste of adventure.

It was a good thing she hadn't started a new relationship yet, because she sure wouldn't have time for one.

Her phone rang. Joe. "Hi," she said, aiming for breezy.

"Kincaid's lined up the appraiser for eleven o'clock. Do you want to be there?"

"Should I be?"

"I can't, so either we reschedule or you'll have to do it. I'll have a copy of the key made for Kincaid."

"I'm at my parents' store. I can do it now, then meet him at the house." She wanted to know why Joe wouldn't be there. He wasn't involved in the labor part of his job anymore, except to do Nana Mae's yard. He drummed up business, designed landscapes, supervised work—surely he could take a half hour to oversee the appraisal. It wasn't like him to give up that kind of control.

"Sounds good, Dix. Thanks. Let me know how it goes, okay?"

"Okay." She hung up. He sounded strange. Strained. As if he was trying to keep himself as upbeat for her as she was for him.

And why the interest earlier in how she felt about Kincaid? What did it matter?

"Is everything okay?" her mother asked.

"What? Oh. Yes, it's fine. In case you start hearing more rumors about Joe and me, here's the truth instead." She disclosed the bare minimum about selling the house, having learned not to take her parents into her confidence unless she wanted an earful of debate that usually left her unsure. She didn't need that now. She needed to be around people who believed in her. It was another reason she wanted them gone for now. Another reason for stretching herself thin.

And then there was another concern niggling at the corners of her mind. If she gave up all ties to Joe, did it mean she would lose his family—who had become her family—too?

Oh, they all might try to stay friends, but she couldn't be invited to the family parties anymore. It wouldn't be right. Yet so much of her social life was tied up with the McCoys—all thirty-five of them.

She didn't even want to think about it. She was going to let herself be excited, and enjoy the process of being just Dixie.

Chapter Four

It had been a very long week, Joe thought, a roller-coaster ride from beginning to end. But right now it was Saturday night, which meant a live band would be playing at the Stompin' Grounds, the local watering hole famous for its beer and burgers for forty years. Joe hadn't missed too many Saturday nights there.

The bar and grill's interior showed its age, but it was rare that someone saw it in full light, anyway, the wagon-wheel-shaped overhead fixtures lighting up the room only enough to see who was crying in their beer or sneaking a kiss. Customers wouldn't tolerate change, not brighter lights or unmarred tabletops or a floor without peanut shells.

Joe leaned against the bar, a mug of draft in hand, remembering his first time at the Stompin' Grounds. He and Dixie turned twenty-one a day apart, he first. His brothers, Jake and Donovan, had made it a point to be home for his birthday, and he was as thrilled to have his big brothers here to help him celebrate as he was to turn twenty-one.

Leaving an underage, unhappy Dixie behind, Jake and Donovan bought Joe his first drink, then his second. His third. And finally his fourth—just in time for Dixie to show up at midnight, legally of age to be here. He hadn't passed out, but he'd been "stupidly happy," as Jake had called him.

Joe felt tempted to repeat that momentous occasion tonight. To make sure he didn't, he'd invited Jake and his wife, Keri, to come with him.

He sipped his first beer of the evening as he watched his brother and sister-in-law dance, enjoying a rare night away from their seven-month-old daughter, Isabella. The jukebox music was slow and twangy. They were wrapped in each other's arms, barely taking up space on the dance floor, seemingly fused together.

Maybe a new McCoy would be conceived tonight. For sure, Joe and Dixie had left here many Saturday nights to tangle in bed, all hot and bothered from dancing body to body. If she hadn't been on the pill…

He wondered if she would show up tonight. It had been their Saturday-night tradition for a long time, one they'd both continued since their breakup, the difference being that they'd been ignoring each other across the crowded room for a year.

She'd brought loan papers for him to sign two days ago. She looked good, rushed but also relaxed. Excited and happy. He hadn't seen her openly happy in a very long time, leading him to conclude he'd done the right thing by officially ending their relationship.

He'd heard she hired Bruno Manning as her contractor, a man with a reputation for good work, but who was always behind schedule. Joe was surprised she hadn't used Kincaid, wondered what was happening with them, if anything.

The band was almost ready to start their first set. They were checking mikes and sound levels over the jukebox music, creating a clamor. Memories assaulted him. It was here, little more than a year ago, with the same band playing, that he'd proposed to Dixie in public.

They'd started off the evening at opposite sides of the room because they'd been fighting for a couple of weeks. She had moved out, in fact, having reached the end of her rope with him. He knew he would lose her if he didn't propose, so he did, in front of everyone. She accepted. They were happy for a few days—until she asked him to set a date.

He'd hesitated, then froze.

If he married her, he would never leave Chance City. If he didn't marry her, there was a possibility someday he would be able to go. He hadn't thought it through. He'd only thought about losing Dixie.

But he'd wanted what his brothers had—the opportunity to see the world, to do something exciting. If he married Dixie, they would start a family right away. It was what she wanted. He couldn't tell her he didn't want that yet. She would think he didn't want *her,* and that wasn't true.

She'd accused him once of wanting to play the field, but that had never been true. It had always been Dixie for him. He'd dated a little when they were separated, but he'd never slept with another woman.

He tried to tell her that, but she'd thrown the ring at him, piled some clothes into a suitcase and taken off. The next day while he was working, she took the rest of her belongings, leaving her key behind on the dining-room table.

That was when he knew this break would be different from the other times. And it had been. Painfully so. And now his brothers had moved home. He would have his chance, after all. The chance to see the world, as they had.

But at what cost?

"Let's get a round in before the band starts," Jake said, breaking into Joe's thoughts and handing him a cue stick.

Joe looked around. "Where's Keri?"

Jake nodded to his wife where she sat at a table with Dixie. Joe had been lost in such a sea of memories that he hadn't seen or heard her come in. Keri glanced over, looking serious, but Dixie was angled sideways.

He did notice Dixie was wearing her lucky red boots, however, and his favorite yellow Western shirt, with

Wranglers that fit like a second skin. He knew how her hair would smell, knew how the curls felt in his hands—

"Let it go," Jake said close to Joe's ear. "The table won't be free for long."

Joe was racking the balls when the door swung open and his brother Donovan and new wife, Laura, breezed in, fresh from their honeymoon.

"Aloha!" Laura shouted.

The drummer sounded a roll, then the lead guitarist played something vaguely Hawaiian sounding. Laura broke into a hula. She and Donovan both looked tanned and rested and happy.

A little envious, Joe made his way to them, waited until everyone was done hugging, then offered to buy the newlyweds a drink.

"We're not staying," Donovan said. "We saw all your cars in the parking lot and thought we'd say hello. But we're anxious to see Ethan. Mom let him stay up. He's waiting."

"What's this I hear about you working for your parents?" Joe heard Laura ask Dixie.

The news came as a shock to Joe. No one had passed on that a bit of information. He looked at Dixie in time to see her shifting her feet in that way she had that signaled she was uncomfortable.

"You were supposed to be in a gossip-free zone during your honeymoon," she said to Laura.

"I talked to Keri every day. She kept Ethan when Aggie couldn't. So, is it true?"

"My parents headed south today in an RV for a little vacation. I'm helping out while they're gone."

"Are you crazy?" Joe asked, unable to hold back. "You hated working for them. With good reason."

Silence descended among the six people huddled together. The band launched into their opening number, causing the floor to shake under their feet, making conversation impossible, too, without yelling.

"They need me," she shouted.

He couldn't tell if she was angry or just making herself heard over the music.

"And I know what I'm doing," she added. "Plus they won't be here, you know. *And* it's really none of your business."

She won't have time to date.

The thought struck him, loud and clear.

Then Kincaid came up beside her, not touching her, but making his presence known. Even without laying a hand on her, he looked proprietary.

Did she have a date with Kincaid? Is that why she'd come without her friends Sheryl and Nancy, her usual companions?

It was what he'd wanted—he'd handpicked Kincaid—but seeing them standing together, smiling at each other…

Joe couldn't stay. It was awkward for all of them, but particularly for him, since he was the one without a date. Although if he'd had a date, he wouldn't have brought her here, to the place where he and Dixie usually could be found every Saturday night.

Why the hell hadn't they gone somewhere else? Why flaunt it?

It hurt. He hadn't expected it to hurt this much.

"I'm glad you're back," Joe said to Donovan and Laura, then he left, his gut filled with the fire of jealousy. He recognized it for what it was, couldn't control it. Could only hope he would get over it with time and distance.

For now, there were places he could go, people he could see....

He went home.

A car was parked in front of his house. He saw someone inside the battered, unfamiliar vehicle. He pulled into his driveway. As he opened his door, a woman climbed out of the car.

"Hi, Joe," she said. She walked around the car and onto the sidewalk. In her arms was a bundle she tucked close. "This is Emma."

"Sorry we're late!" Sheryl said, rushing up to Dixie at the Stompin' Grounds.

"My fault, totally," Nancy added. "Next round's on me. We'll go get a pitcher."

Dixie was in no mood to stay. Donovan and Laura had left a minute after Joe. Jake and Keri were dancing, but looked like they should find a bed somewhere. Kincaid was off ordering a hamburger rather than waiting for the waitress to show up.

Dixie didn't know what to do about him. She hadn't told him she would be here, but almost everyone in town knew she came most Saturday nights, so it wasn't a stretch for him to come by if he was looking for her.

Her new life wasn't starting off as well as she'd anticipated. She shouldn't even be here tonight, she had so much work to do. Most importantly, she had to get her apartment in order tomorrow, before the workweek started. Without a settled home base in place, her life would be chaotic.

Sheryl and Nancy would help, but she also needed a truck to carry her furniture from Joe's house—the bedroom set from the guest room that had been hers from high school, her great-grandmother's rocking chair, a small desk. The china cabinet. She could buy new, but these were pieces with sentimental value—sentiments that wouldn't matter to Joe. Maybe he even wanted to get rid of everything. She hadn't asked him where he planned to live.

She wished he hadn't taken off, wasn't sure why he had, except that she could tell he'd been surprised by the news she was helping her parents. Maybe even disgusted with her for agreeing?

She wanted to assure him that she was a different woman now. That her parents wouldn't get to her the way they used to. Wouldn't make her feel guilty for spending less time with them than she had with the McCoys.

Dixie might as well be an only child. She knew her parents expected more of her because she'd never left Chance City, unlike her brother and sister. Her parents depended on her. Leaned on her. She'd allowed it for a long time.

"Sure you're not hungry?" Kincaid asked, setting his plate on the table, along with a big basket of fries.

And why was he sitting down as if she'd invited him?

Sheryl and Nancy would be thrilled, however. They'd talked about him before, wondered why he never was seen around town in the evening. Not that there was a lot of nightlife beyond the diner....

Kincaid nudged the fries a little closer.

"I'm okay, thanks," she said, although they did smell delicious. And maybe she was just a little hungry. But now that she'd turned him down, how could she grab some?

"Band's good," he said.

She nodded. "I don't think I've ever seen you here before."

"I saw your car in the parking lot and took a chance. Now I see what I've been missing."

Was it as simple as that? He was a smart man, one who calculated potential success for every project he got involved with. Was she his new project?

She moved away from him a little, uncertain.

He lifted his burger, eyed her, then said, "I'll eat and run."

She felt guilty. No one liked to eat alone. "It's fine, really. If you don't mind sharing the table with Sheryl and Nancy." She watched them make their way back, their hands full.

Redheaded Nancy grinned. "Well, hey, Kincaid. Fancy meeting you here."

"Hi, Nancy. Sheryl, how're you?"

If he was disappointed he wasn't going to be alone with Dixie, he didn't show it. Every so often, his shoulder bumped hers, or his foot under the table, but the space was crowded. And she finally did snag a few fries. He didn't say anything, didn't even tease her, as most people would.

When the table was cleared, she expected him to leave. Instead he invited her to dance. He was a good dancer. She'd learned that at the wedding. There was no reason not to, except that Jake and Keri were still there and would see.

So?

Her cell phone vibrated in her pocket before she could answer either Kincaid or her conscience. *Joe.* Now what? She wished she could just ignore it.

"I need to take this call," she said, pressing the talk button and heading to the door at the same time. "Hold on. I'll be in the parking lot in a second," she said into the phone. As soon as the door closed behind her, she said hello.

"You need to come to the house," he said. "Now."

"What's wrong?"

"You'll see. No one's hurt, Dix. Don't speed. But you need to come."

"All right." She clenched the phone and went inside to make her apologies. Kincaid followed her to her car.

"You're upset," he said. "I could drive you. Get someone to take your car home."

"He said no one was hurt. I'm more curious than

worried." Which wasn't entirely true. He wouldn't call her about something that wasn't major.

Kincaid put a hand on her arm before she started the engine. "Look, Dixie. I know this is a transition time for you. Everyone is talking about it," he added when she frowned. "I haven't been prying, but one meal at the Lode is all it took. All I'm saying is, I'm not a McCoy, I'm a good listener and I want to be your friend. So, call me, night or day, if you need to, okay?"

"Yeah. Thanks. I have to go."

He backed away. The ten-minute drive to her— *Joe's*—house seemed to take an hour. She parked behind a car she didn't recognize, rushed up the walkway. The door opened before she could knock. Joe stood there, but he moved aside.

Dixie's heart slammed into her ribs. "Shana," she said. Her kid sister, who'd run away almost eleven years ago.

"Hey, Dix." She had the same smile, but set in a much-too-gaunt face.

A sound intruded. A baby crying. Shana moved to pick up the swaddled bundle on the sofa, nestled by pillows on all sides.

"This is Emma. My daughter."

Chapter Five

"I can stay at my mom's," Joe said to Dixie an hour later. "You can take my room."

He'd gone to the Lode, picked up some vegetable soup, homemade bread and apple pie for Shana. He hadn't seen a person devour food like that, as if she hadn't eaten for a week, then she'd fallen asleep sitting at the table.

Dixie had eased her into bed in the guest room, set up the porta-crib they kept stowed in the laundry room and put the four-month-old to bed, too. Joe had gone out to Shana's car and brought in her belongings, which weren't much.

"I appreciate the offer, Joe," Dixie said, "but I'll sleep

on the couch, if you don't mind. If you want to stay at your mom's anyway, I understand, but you don't need to give up your room. I'll take care of everything tomorrow. It'll only be for tonight."

"She looks bad, Dix."

Dixie nodded, her eyes tearing up. "She's been through some kind of hell." She reached for his hand and squeezed. "Thank you for everything."

He didn't let go, wanting to hold her, wanting to take care of her, as natural a thing as breathing. "I'll be going out of town tomorrow. She can stay. You both can stay for a few days, if you want."

"For once, her timing is perfect." She let go and then sat on the couch, her hands clenched. "With Mom and Dad having left this morning, their house is available."

He sat on the couch, too, a few feet away. "You're going to ask their permission first, right?" Shana was the black sheep, the ungrateful daughter. Joe didn't think Bea and Malcolm would be pleased to have her stay at their house.

"If I ask them, they'll come home."

"Isn't that the point? Shouldn't they have that option? They haven't seen or talked to her, either."

"I think Shana would just take off again, right away. I'm going to try to convince her to stay long enough to see Mom and Dad. But not yet, okay?" Dixie held his gaze. "You remember how Shana operates. She never lets her roots go deep. So, chances are, she'll rest, get some good food in her, sweet-talk me into giving her some money and be gone again. I'll get a Christmas card without a return address, as usual, but always post-marked from a new city."

"It's your call. But don't you think your parents' neighbors will alert them?"

"You know my mom and dad, Joe. No technology for them, even though it would save them a lot of time. So, no cell phone. They'll be calling me, but that's all."

"All right. But my mom would be happy to put them up. Mother them."

"I know, thanks. I need more information from Shana first. What if she's involved in something criminal? What if she's on the run? I can't subject your mom to that possibility."

"Or yourself, Dix."

"She's my sister."

Joe understood the familial bond, but he'd also never had to deal with a sibling gone wrong. All of his brothers and sisters lived in Chance City now. All were happily married with children. They helped each other out, however, no matter what the issue.

He patted Dixie's shoulder. "I'll get some bedding for you." Emotion swirled in him. He'd gone from jealous to angry to worried in a few heartbeats. He wouldn't fall asleep for hours, probably, but would be stuck in his bedroom, killing time.

"I won't be able to sleep yet," she said. "Unless you've moved things, I'll get a pillow and blanket when I'm ready. I know where to find everything." She looked out the window. "I'm wondering if we should move her car into the garage, out of sight. Is there space?"

His truck was too big for the small garage attached to the eighty-year-old house, but Shana's car would fit. "Good thinking. I'll do it."

The cold night air felt good, the cranked-up heat in the house having become stifling. He drew in a deep breath, filled his lungs until he coughed. Shana had come to his house looking for Dixie, which meant she hadn't known they'd split up a year ago. She'd been visibly shocked.

"If you two can't make it, who can?" she'd asked wearily.

Good question. McCoys *made* it. That was about as close to a commandment as was possible, outside the Bible. No McCoy had divorced, ever, nor had a child out of wedlock, although there'd been some close calls.

Joe moved the cars around, taking his time. He was in no hurry. Having Dixie here—just when he'd gotten used to her not being here—was harder than he'd ever imagined.

"Dix?" he said when he finally went inside again, not seeing her.

She came through the dining-room door, wiping her hands, apparently having been cleaning up the dishes.

"I think we've got another problem," he said. "*Your* car. I don't think it should be out front overnight, either." Because so much had happened during the evening, it seemed late, but it wasn't even ten o'clock. Lots of people would drive by. Neighbors would notice.

Dixie put a hand to her mouth. "You're right. I'll take it to Nana Mae's and then walk back. I should tell her what's going on, anyway."

"I'll do it. Just give me your keys. You should be here if Shana wakes up—or the baby. I wouldn't know what to do."

Dixie grinned, the sight unexpected. "You would, too. No man I know deals with babies as well as you. You're Super Uncle. But I'll accept your offer, thanks." She dug into her pocket for her keys and passed them to him, their hands brushing. "You said you're leaving town tomorrow. Where are you going?"

"A little town near Burbank. I have a meeting with a group of city officials about how to start a community-compost business like I started here." It would be his first flight. Hard to imagine that he was thirty years old and hadn't flown anywhere before. "Can you believe it? People want to pay me to tell them how to make fertilizer."

"I can believe it," she said, her smile soft. She hadn't looked at him with tenderness for so long, he wasn't sure how to react. He wanted to hold her, just hold her. To tuck his face into her neck, to feel her breasts and hips align with his. To kiss her—

His body reacted to the image. He spun on his heel, headed to the door, but stopped there, his hand on the knob, his back to her. "I won't be long. Is there anything else you think she might need?"

"I'd say there's plenty, but we'll deal with it tomorrow. I should probably call Gavin…. No, not yet. I need to know more about what we're dealing with first. My brother is a busy man."

"And you're not busy?" She was always the first one to volunteer, the last one to leave after cleaning up. He'd learned to accept that about her, because it was part of who she was. But she had a whole lot on her plate these days.

"She's my sister, Joe. You'd do the same for one of yours."

"Yeah." He couldn't fault the argument. "Will Nana Mae be up or asleep, do you suppose?"

"She'll be up for another hour or so."

"Anything you need?"

"A pair of pajamas from my dresser would be great."

He didn't want to dwell on how personal that would be. He'd handled her clothes plenty of times. Her body, too.

"I won't be long." Once again the cold air was a reprieve, as the trip tomorrow would be, too. His life had suddenly gone from predictable to unpredictable.

He'd been looking for change in his life. It seemed he was about to get it.

"She has the Callahan green eyes," Dixie said, seated in her great-grandmother's rocking chair and looking into her niece's eyes as she sucked down a bottle of formula. She'd awakened the moment Joe had left.

"Those are strong genes." Shana tucked an afghan more tightly around herself as she sat on the sofa, watching. Dark circles under her eyes made her look haggard. "I know you're curious, Dix. I'm not ready to talk yet."

"Just tell me this much. Are you on the run? Will someone be tracking you down? I need to know if you're in some kind of danger, or us, for that matter, because that will change how things are handled."

"No. No cops, either."

Dixie relaxed. Emma smiled, formula pooling around her mouth. "She's adorable."

"She deserves more than I can give her."

Joe came through the door before Dixie could respond to the statement. Was that why Shana had come? To drop off her baby, unable to care for her?

He set a grocery sack next to the couch. "Nana Mae added a few more things she thought you might need. You didn't sleep long," Joe said to Shana as he headed to the fireplace.

"Emma has her own schedule. After this feeding, she'll be good until six tomorrow morning or so. I just told Dixie—you don't have to worry about anything, where I'm concerned. I haven't done anything criminal."

"Glad to hear that."

Shana bristled. "I've *never* been in any kind of serious trouble."

Although surprised at Joe's parental tone, and fighting her instinct to defend her sister, Dixie decided to let him lead the conversation. He could probably get more out of Shana than she could. Shana had always adored him. In many ways he'd been more of a brother than Gavin had.

"Doesn't look like it to me," Joe said, looking over

his shoulder. "Seems like you haven't done a good job of taking care of yourself, either."

"Well, I was smart enough to get myself where I would be, wasn't I?"

Her words left a hollow sound in the air, an uncomfortable silence.

"Why are you letting him talk to me that way?" Shana asked Dixie, her voice pitched high.

Joe made a sound of frustration.

"He's being honest, Shana. Why would I interfere with that?" Dixie kept her tone even and her voice hushed as Emma's eyes drifted shut. Her mouth went lax around the bottle's nipple. Dixie moved her onto her shoulder and rubbed her back. Such a sweet little girl to be living a life of unknowns. "But you're right, too. You're here now, where you know people will be willing to help you, *glad* to help you. Don't take advantage of that generosity."

Shana stared at the floor, her shoulders set, her jaw like marble. Finally, she nodded. "I need a shower. Is that okay? Do you mind watching Emma?"

"I don't mind at all."

Dixie continued to rock the baby. When the shower came on, she asked Joe what Nana Mae's reaction was.

"She remembers what Shana was like as a teenager. Did she open up about her life at all, what she's been doing all these years?"

"No. But that's not surprising, is it? She always kept to herself."

"To her detriment. Do you think you can sleep now?" he asked.

Light danced across his face from the fireplace flames. Such a good man. Such a very good man. He'd always shouldered everyone else's burdens, particularly after his father died. And here he was again, taking on responsibilities that weren't his. He must be pleased to be leaving, getting away from all those responsibilities.

"Thank you," she said, her voice shaky.

"For what?"

"For being you." She didn't want to continue the conversation, was afraid of undoing all she'd done to get over him. "I'll put the baby down and change for bed in the guest room."

"It'd make me happier if you'd sleep in my bed."

She shook her head. Too many memories. Too much temptation, too.

By the time Shana was out of the shower, Joe had retreated to his room. Dixie stretched out on the couch, where she could watch the dying fire, and listen to the occasional crackle or spark.

After a while she closed her eyes. A door opened. Someone padded quietly down the hall. Joe came into the living room, then hesitated.

"I'm awake," she said, noticing he wore the flannel robe she'd given him years ago. She remembered how cozy it felt to the touch.

She should have made him go to his mother's for the night….

She wanted him.

"You can't sleep, either?" he said.

"Adrenaline rush aftermath," she said, sitting up, glad he couldn't see the need in her eyes. "I think I'm still in shock, seeing her again. And I have questions."

"Yeah." He moved to the fire, stoked it, added a large log. "How about some hot chocolate?"

She shouldn't be alone with him. She really shouldn't. "Good idea." She started to get up.

"I'll do it. Enjoy the fire."

It was cozy, sitting and watching the flames, listening to the sound of him making cocoa. It brought back so many sweet memories. She laid her head against her upraised knees, remembering the first night they'd moved in. Boxes were everywhere, their furniture hand-me-downs and garage-sale finds. But it was theirs, and they were beyond happy.

Before they'd gone to bed, she remembered he'd made hot chocolate that night, too. They'd curled up on the sofa to watch the fire. They'd just turned twenty-one, had already been going steady for seven years. Lots of people disapproved of them buying a house and living together without marriage, especially her parents, Joe's mom and Nana Mae. Even her brother had his say about it.

Dixie had felt the same, to a lesser degree, but she knew how much Joe loved her, knew he would propose one day. He had, eight years later. It lasted five days.

"What are you thinking?" Joe asked, bringing her

back to the present, passing her a mug, then sitting on the sofa a few feet away.

"That life's not fair." She raised her mug in thanks, then took a sip. "Perfect temperature, as always. You're the cocoa master."

"What's not fair, Dix?"

She could see a sliver of his chest where his robe gaped a little, firelight flickering on his flesh, and his legs, bare from the knees down. She ached to run her hands along them, to feel the static electricity the hair on his legs would create. She wanted to spread her hands over his chest, push the flannel aside, kiss him there....

"What's not fair?" he repeated.

She stalled by taking another sip of cocoa. "I was supposed to move into my apartment tomorrow. I won't have time now. It'll probably take most of the day getting Shana and Emma settled." She sighed. "It's petty of me, isn't it? Shana's been through hell, and I'm annoyed by having to delay my plans for one day. Selfish."

"Dix, you are the least selfish person I know. I think you've figured out the impact that Shana's being here is going to have. She's always been demanding. Always. You can't let her get to you. You've already taken on a big load." He raised a hand. "I know. I know. It's none of my business."

"No, you're right. I could easily get stressed out and then fall apart. I need to be careful, look to the future. At some point the salon will be renovated. My parents will return. Shana will either get settled or leave. Everything will be okay. Provided the loan is approved."

"When will you hear about that?"

"On Monday, I hope."

"Dix."

She heard hesitation in his voice. "What?" What was he reluctant to say?

"If they won't give you the loan, I'd be happy to bankroll you. I'm making a whole lot of money these days."

She couldn't keep that kind of connection with him, no matter how considerate the offer was. "I appreciate the offer, Joe. I really do. But I have a backup plan already."

"Kincaid, I'll bet."

"What makes you say that?" How could he possibly know?

"Lucky guess. How'd he take it when you had to leave tonight?"

She frowned. "He offered to drive me here. What was there for him to *take?*"

"Weren't you on a date with him?"

His seemingly casual tone blared in her head. He was jealous. At first she was flattered, then she changed her mind. It would take a long time for the intense emotions they'd felt for each other through the years to find a soft place to land.

She leaned forward and laid a hand on his shoulder. "Do you honestly think I'd show up on a Saturday night at the Stompin' Grounds with a *date?*"

"He likes you."

"I can tell."

"He'd be good for you. To you."

"Probably so. I'm not ready." She let her hand drop away and immediately missed the warmth, his strength. It would be so easy to go to bed with him. But then what? They wouldn't be back to square one, exactly, but maybe starting at a different place on the game board instead, without any instructions on how to play the game.

Just as Nana Mae had given Dixie wings, so Dixie needed to give Joe wings, too.

Because she had the feeling if she made any move toward coming back to him, he wouldn't do what he needed to do—and he would always regret it. She wouldn't be responsible for that.

"I think we're both having a hard time with the finality of this, Joe," she said. "But we both also know it's what we need to do."

He nodded. An explosion of sparks burst in the fireplace, as if adding its agreement.

"Where will you live after the house sells?" she asked.

"I'll figure it out when it happens." He tilted his mug, finishing the warm drink. "Done?" he asked.

"Not quite."

He went into the kitchen then said good-night as he passed through again, heading to his bedroom. Alone.

"I love you, Joe," she whispered into the night. "Forever."

Peace came over her, warm and soothing. She

wouldn't fight her love for him anymore. She'd had to fight it for an entire year, the only way she could've survived the separation. But now she faced the truth— she would never stop loving him.

She didn't have to, either. She could just hold that love close, and find pleasure in her work, her friends, her family.

She closed her eyes and felt sleep begin to take hold, all the fight gone from her.

She'd never expected to see the day when the fight was gone.

It felt good.

Chapter Six

"I'm not staying at Mom and Dad's," Shana said the next morning, while devouring a stack of pancakes drenched in butter and maple syrup, and a tall glass of milk.

"You don't have a choice—unless you can pay for a hotel." Dixie brought her own plate to the table and sat across from her sister. Shana looked better. Having a shower helped, but so had a good night's sleep.

She waved a piece of bacon at Dixie. "Joe said I could stay here while he's gone."

"You're not doing that," Dixie stated flatly, but smiled at sweet little Emma in her baby seat on the table, waving her hands, kicking her feet and babbling.

Joe had been gone since dawn. He'd told her he would leave for the airport around two o'clock.

"Who made you boss?" Shana asked, pouting.

"You came to me for help. I'm helping."

Shana shoved her long, straight hair out of her face and blew out a breath. "I know. I'm sorry. It's just… Mom and Dad? You *know?*"

"I do know. But at least you'll have privacy. How long do you plan to stay?" Dixie asked as if the answer wasn't important.

"I don't know."

"Well, this time when you leave, will you please let me know you're going?"

"I promise."

"You need a haircut." She obviously hadn't had a professional cut in ages. Partly grown-out bangs fell into her eyes all the time—although that also came from hanging her head a lot, allowing her hair to curtain her face, and hide her expression. The rest lay like a limp blanket down her back.

Shana touched her hair self-consciously. "Will you do it? You were always good at that."

"I'd be happy to." She dragged a pad of paper close to her. "Let's make a shopping list."

After cleaning up the kitchen, Dixie walked to Nana Mae's house to retrieve her car, grateful Nana Mae would be at church and not there to ask questions that Dixie couldn't answer yet. After doing the grocery shopping, they would come back for Shana's less reliable car, and later go to the consignment shop for clothes, but it didn't open until noon on Sunday.

The fact that Shana was okay with being in public relaxed Dixie about Shana's reasons for being on the run, although it didn't rule out her baby's father as a possible reason. Maybe he'd been abusive, and she was hiding from him. Maybe he was married. Maybe Shana didn't even know who the father was.

All Dixie knew for sure was that Shana was running, but whether it was to or from something, Dixie didn't know.

"Man," Shana said as they walked through the door of their parents' house later. "This is weird. Like some kind of time warp. What a cave. Was it always so dark?"

"Nothing's changed," Dixie said, setting two grocery sacks on the kitchen counter and eyeing the old, dark paneling and drapes. "Except your room. It's Mom's sewing room now."

"Mom sews?"

"No, but that's what it's called. You can use my bedroom."

"Which has been left as a shrine to you, I imagine," Shana said, bitterness in her voice.

"Pretty much, except I took my furniture, so yours is in my room. For the first six months after Joe and I broke up, I came back here to live. It was like stepping into an episode of *The Twilight Zone*. I'll get the rest of your things." Dixie wasn't about to apologize for her parents' behavior. Shana chose to run away, chose not to communicate. After years passed without contact, she'd become dead to them. It was the only way they could cope. If she hadn't sent a Christmas card every year to Dixie, no one would've known she was even alive.

"Even Gavin's room is the same," Shana said when Dixie tracked her down a few minutes later, the groceries put away. She held her daughter, who was awake and looking around. "What's he up to?"

"He's in San Francisco. He's a doctor."

"So he made it, after all. Good for him."

"He was determined. Take a guess what he specializes in."

Shana frowned, then her eyes took on some sparkle. "Gynecology?"

"You got it."

"Lover boy to the end."

Dixie laughed, was grateful for a moment that seemed normal between them. Emma smiled, too, wriggling happily. Dixie ran a hand over the infant's downy head.

"What about her father?" Dixie asked.

The entire mood of the moment changed. Dixie knew it would, but had to ask anyway.

"He died."

Shana had hesitated long enough before answering that Dixie questioned her honesty. Maybe she was after sympathy—or maybe she was hiding something. She had always been secretive.

"You don't believe me," Shana said now, bouncing

Emma in her arms as she began to fuss, probably picking up on the tension.

"Do you blame me?"

After a few beats, Shana shrugged. "You don't really know me anymore, though, do you?" Before Dixie could answer, Shana brushed past her, saying, "I need to fix a bottle for Emma."

"I'll do it," Dixie said.

Shana put out an arm, stopping her. "No. *I* will. I'm her mother, not you. And you're not *my* mother, either, Dixie. Believe it or not, I'm actually fairly competent about most things."

Although startled, Dixie was also glad to see her spirit emerge. "Do you want me to leave? Do you want to go clothes shopping without me? I would understand that." And it would give her time to move some of her things into her new apartment.

"No." Shana drew a shaky breath. "I'm sorry. I'm touchy, I know. I really want to spend time with you. Plus, there's another issue, I hate to admit."

"You're broke."

"I'll pay you back, I promise. Or work it off somehow. You're still working for Mom and Dad, I guess, which leaves that out. But is there anything else I can help you with?"

She looked eager and sincere. But with Shana, looks could be deceiving. "I'm helping Mom and Dad at the store while they're gone," Dixie said. "But I'm doing something entirely different now. I'll show you later. For the moment, do you want to rest for a while after you feed Emma?" She looked at her watch. "The stores are opening about now."

"I don't need to rest. But can we walk?" she asked. "I'd really like to walk. We can put anything we buy in the stroller."

"Sounds good to me."

They spent hours shopping, greeting people, letting Emma be admired. Not everyone remembered Shana, but because she belonged to Dixie, she was welcomed warmly.

The McCoys were curiously absent around town, but then, it was Sunday, so they were probably having a family dinner, which happened more often than not. Dixie ignored the tug at her heart, the wish to be in the middle of the fracas that was a McCoy family occasion.

The Callahan women finally ended up at Bitty's Beauty Shoppe as dark settled in. "One last stop," Dixie said, sliding her key in the lock, inviting her sister and niece inside. "Welcome to the future home of the Respite Spa and Salon, Dixie Callahan, owner."

Shana's eyes lit up, more animated than she'd been all day. "Really? You bought it?"

"Almost. The loan is still in the works, but I have so many plans, Shana. So many plans."

"That's good, because this place needs to be demolished and started over."

"It will be. And the big bonus—it comes with an apartment upstairs. Want to see it?"

"Absolutely." Shana lifted a sleeping Emma from the stroller and carried her up the staircase.

"I didn't want to move in until I'd gotten everything painted and window coverings up," Dixie said as she reached the landing, unlocked the entry door and reached for the light switch. "So, it's empty at the moment, but by next week—"

She stopped. Stared. Moved slowly into the room.

"Looks done to me," Shana said behind her.

Not done, exactly, but all the things she'd wanted from Joe's house were here, and a few extra items, although still plenty to buy that would be her own choices. She moved into the kitchen. There were dry goods in the pantry, her refrigerator filled to capacity.

Trancelike, she went into the bedroom. Her new bedspread was on her bed, the one from Joe's guest room, her clothes from Nana Mae's house hung in the closet.

From atop the bedspread, she picked up an envelope, a Congratulations on Your New Home card, the note in Nana Mae's handwriting: "It was Joe's idea. Feel free to change anything. We won't be offended. We just wanted to get it all here for you. Love from all the McCoy family—and I do mean *all* the McCoys, old and young."

Dixie dropped onto the bed, the note crushed in her fist.

"What's wrong? What is it?" Shana asked.

She wrapped her arm around Dixie as her tears flowed, hot and heavy. She'd broken up with one of their own, yet they'd done this for her. She loved them all so much.

"What have I done? Why did I give him up? It means I lose them, too. How am I supposed to survive that? They've been part of me almost my whole life, been here for me when Mom and Dad weren't. Had faith in me when Mom and Dad said I couldn't do something, couldn't succeed."

"You didn't give him up, Dix. You let him go. Big difference."

Dixie swiped her cheeks, but tears continued to flow. Shana didn't—couldn't—understand that bond. "Right."

"They're good people. No one denies that," Shana continued, grabbing a tissue from Emma's diaper bag and shoving it at Dixie. "But you don't marry a family. You marry a man. And that man wasn't—isn't—husband material."

Dixie drew a shaky breath. "You're right. I know you are. And I know it's over. It had to be over."

"I hear a but in there."

She faced her sister. "But I can't seem to stop loving him. What if I never do? What if I can never fall in love with someone else? I want children. I want a home and family, Shana. What if—"

"Oh, get a grip, Dix. You're thirty years old, not ninety. What happened to the take-no-prisoners Dixie I remember? When did you lose yourself?"

Dixie realized how pitiful she'd sounded. She climbed off the bed, tossed her tissue into a pretty wastebasket she'd picked up on her shopping trip to Sacramento on Sunday. She reminded herself that she'd found peace last night while deciding to just let herself love him. That it was okay.

And it was.

"It seems to me you've found some new dreams," Shana said. "You're starting your own business and building it the way you want it. What do you need a man for, anyway?" Shana bounced Emma, who'd started to cry. "All they do is cause heartache."

Shana's words pulled Dixie out of her own meltdown. "Did he get you pregnant and leave you?" she asked.

"Who?"

"*Who?* Emma's father, of course. I assume he is a man who caused you heartache."

"I told you. He died. I'm just talking about life in general, men in general. I've been around, you know."

"So you said. To Paris for a year. London. Amsterdam. Athens. Rome. I can't even remember everywhere. You've lived in youth hostels and barns—"

"And four-star hotels, don't forget." She scooped up the diaper bag. "I need to fix Emma a bottle."

In the kitchen Dixie heated some of Aggie's pot roast. Joe's mother made the best comfort food, traditional foods, prepared well.

After dinner, Dixie took Shana downstairs and cut her hair. A new woman emerged. Dixie cut off ten inches, so that the blond tresses brushed Shana's shoulders as she moved. Her face opened up, her eyes seeming larger and brighter—and filled with tears.

"Thank you," she whispered.

Dixie hugged her, then didn't let go for a long time, not until Shana finally relaxed into the embrace.

The night was cold and dark by the time Shana and Emma had been delivered home and Dixie returned to her new apartment. All hers. For the first time.

She wandered around, opening cupboards, checking to see what was put where, discovering cleaning products and equipment, jars of herbs and spices, even a used tackle box stocked with basic tools and hardware. Her framed photographs and art were stacked in a cardboard box, awaiting her decision on where to put them. She needed to buy a couch, a dining room table and chairs, an entertainment unit. She needed a rug so the hardwood floors wouldn't seem cold during the winter.

For now, she could live with it.

But it was quiet. She hadn't arranged for cable TV yet, so there was no sense turning it on. She could take a bubble bath.

Instead she pulled her cell phone from her pocket and called Joe. He answered on the second ring.

"Hey," he said.

"Thank you."

"You're welcome. However, I didn't do much of the work because I had to leave."

"It's because of you that it happened. I can't tell you how it made me feel." She climbed onto her bed, relaxed into the pillows. "Please thank your family for me."

"You don't intend to?"

She clutched the phone. "I've been thinking I need to limit my contact with them."

"Dixie, you love them. They love you."

"Yes, on both counts. I'm not saying I won't see them, just that I need to step away a little. You know why, Joe. You do."

"My sisters-in-law are two of your best friends. Your friendship predates their marriages."

"It gets complicated, doesn't it?" Yes, Keri and Laura were good friends. Dixie didn't know how she would resolve that situation. "Where are you?"

"In a hotel by the Burbank airport."

"How was your flight?"

"It was strange. Everyone seemed so laid-back. I suppose I was the only one on the plane who'd never flown before. I was glad when it landed."

She smiled. She'd flown a couple of times. She'd felt exactly the same.

"Then there was the whole rental car business," he said. "I suppose it'll get easy with practice."

It had been a long time since they'd had such a normal conversation.

"How'd things go with Shana?" he asked.

"Not bad. She hasn't confided about Emma's father yet."

"She needs to learn to trust again, just like you."

He was absolutely right. "Well, I won't keep you," she said. "I just wanted to thank you for what you did for me."

"Enjoy your first night."

They hung up. She brushed her hand along the empty spot beside her on the bed. At Nana Mae's she'd slept in a twin bed. She could sprawl in this one.

She decided to take that bubble bath, after all. Before she got up, however, she dialed Aggie McCoy, who had borne and raised the thoughtful Joe. Now sixty-eight, she'd been widowed for almost eleven years, a beautiful, generous, gregarious woman with bottle-black hair and the kindest heart ever.

Dixie hated that Joe's family would be caught in the middle of their split. She didn't want anyone to take sides. Joe was theirs, and that was that.

"Hi, it's Dixie," she said when Aggie answered the phone.

"Hi, sweetheart. How're you?"

Just the sound of her voice had Dixie's heart breaking. "I'm grateful and stunned and happy. Thank you so much."

"It was Joe's idea."

Dixie smiled at how everyone gave Joe the credit, as if fighting the fight for him. "But I know you. You ran the show. Please tell everyone thanks, okay?"

"Why, Dixie Callahan. You know how we thank people in our family."

You give a party, that's how. And everyone brings a dish to share and helps clean up. Dixie didn't know how she could do that.

"You're not divorcing us, you know, Dixie." Aggie's voice had gone soft. "You know how it is for the McCoys."

No babies out of wedlock and no divorces. Yes, she knew the McCoy legacy. Everyone knew. "I'm not a McCoy. And you know darn well that things will get complicated at some point."

"You know what they say about crossing bridges when we come to them. But consider this. Every McCoy except Isabella is a client of yours, and it won't be long before that sweet baby is one. That's thirty-four-plus customers you would lose. Can you afford that?"

It would never come down to money. Dixie knew that, knew that Aggie was just teasing her. "You all get a family discount."

"Well, I sure don't want to lose that!"

"Okay."

"Okay? We're good? No more talk of leaving the family?"

"We're good." The rest she couldn't promise.

"So, when's the party?"

Dixie laughed. "Soon. I promise."

"I hear Shana's back in town. And she's got a little one."

Dixie didn't want any lectures about Shana or stretching herself too thin or taking care not to be taken advantage of. "Emma. She's four months old and adorable."

"How about inviting them to Thanksgiving dinner? I know your folks are out of town."

Dixie hadn't thought that far ahead, although it was only four days. "Thank you, but—"

"Dixie," Aggie said, her voice steady. "You know

what Thanksgiving is like here. All the strays come, all the ones whose family live too far away to see, or who don't have any family at all to share the day with. We've never had fewer than fifty people. Come."

"I'll think about it."

"You know I'll send the boys over to hog-tie you, so you might as well plan on it now."

"All right. All right. Uncle."

"That's better. See? We've already made it past the awkward first phone call. It'll get easier."

Dixie didn't think so, but she decided right at that moment to take things a day at a time. She wasn't going to make promises she couldn't keep or worry about things she couldn't change. She was done crying. She was done fearing what she might lose.

It was Dixie Callahan's Life, Act Two. Intermission over. On with the show.

Chapter Seven

Joe eyed the chaos that was Thanksgiving at his mother's house. Having just arrived, he made his way to the kitchen, where laughter and conversation spilled out, the tones all feminine, the air fragrant with roasting turkey. The room was large enough to hold all the women of his family plus extras, all weaving around each other like bees in a hive, his mother its queen.

Aggie spotted Joe in the kitchen doorway. "There's my baby boy now," she said. Everyone else greeted him, then went back to their tasks. Aggie swept him into a fierce hug. "When did you get back?"

"Late last night. Everything smells good, Mom." And every aroma was a memory of Thanksgivings past.

"How'd it go?" Aggie asked.

"Good. Excellent, in fact." He'd been hired as official consultant to guide the small city through the process of creating a community-wide compost program like the model he'd created in Chance City. He'd stayed a day longer than he'd expected to help put together a grant for funds to get started, as he'd done in his hometown, the first step in his sudden rise in status, professionally and financially.

Aggie leaned close. "I invited Kincaid, just like you asked."

"Thanks."

"I've asked him before, you know, because he always seemed to be alone, but he had some excuse every time. This time he couldn't say yes fast enough."

No surprise there. "Did Dixie come?" He hadn't seen her yet. Usually she could be found in the middle of the hive, her golden hair like a spotlight, making her instantly visible.

"She's getting the cranberry sauce out of the garage refrigerator. She could probably use some help," she said, her expression unusually blank.

Joe resisted the temptation. "She'll holler if she does. Anything I can do?"

"You've done more than your share for years."

"Idle hands, you know," he said with a grin. Everyone worked, and even the three-year-olds had tasks to do.

"Your brothers are lighting the outdoor heaters. Go help them. We'll be carving the turkeys pretty soon.

Wait. Hang on a sec." She opened an ice chest and pulled out a beer. "Here."

He found Jake and Donovan watching the littlest kids clamoring over the play structure in the backyard. The heaters were lit, keeping the covered patio warm enough for guests to escape the crush inside the house.

Joe loved having his brothers home for good—not because it had freed him to go off himself, but because they weren't just brothers, but great friends, too. Jake, seven years older than Joe, had spent years on the road doing specialized security work. Donovan, four years younger than Jake, was an acclaimed photojournalist who'd gotten his kicks out of being in the thick of the action, whether wars or protest marches or peace sit-ins.

And now they'd both found the loves of their lives and different, less risky jobs to do, and had come home to love their wives and raise their children.

The McCoy genes dominated in the three brothers. People often commented on how much they looked alike, which was one of the reasons why Joe had grown his hair long as a teenager and kept it that way. He wanted to be seen as different.

"The conqueror returns," Donovan said, spotting him, pounding his back in greeting. "How does it feel to do a job that doesn't get dirt under your nails?"

"Weird, actually." He'd never minded getting dirty. He loved working the soil, seeing what he could coax from nothing but dirt, seeds and water. "I've worked ten times harder for one-tenth the money."

Jake tapped his bottle of beer to Joe's. "What'd I tell you?"

"That people will pay well for expertise. You were right. How's everything been here?"

"I haven't seen Dixie all week," Donovan said, purposely narrowing the question to the person he thought Joe was really interested in.

"Me, either," added Jake.

"I'm right here." Dixie came up beside them, her arms wrapped around a tub of homemade cranberry sauce.

"Let me get that," Joe said, passing his beer to Jake and reaching for the container.

"I've got it, thanks. These muscles haven't atrophied from disuse yet."

One thing they'd done together through the years was work out. And she'd been a wrestler in high school. He'd always found her physical strength sexy.

"Did you have a good trip?" she asked.

She seemed to be forcing herself to be friendly. Her lips were smiling, but her eyes weren't. "Yeah, thanks."

"Kincaid has papers for you to sign, when you've got time. I already have."

"No problem."

She headed to the back door just as Kincaid came out. They exchanged a few words, then he took the tub from her and followed her inside. Into the silence that descended over the brothers came Keri and Laura, who stumbled outside, laughing, each racing to her own husband and hugging him.

"Our first McCoy Thanksgiving," Keri said, her eyes sparkling. "What a zoo. Tell Laura and me that you get used to it."

"Get used to what?" Donovan asked.

"The noise. The activity. The crazi… Oh," Laura said. "You were teasing."

He looked blankly at his brothers. "Is it noisy here? Crazy?"

"I don't see it," Jake said, looking around.

Joe smiled, but he also envied his brothers having wives to tease, to nestle against them and close their eyes as if napping standing up.

You could have that.

Yes, he could, but at what cost? Regret would haunt him, which would make him a bad husband in the long run.

Kincaid joined them. "Wow," he said, a bewildered look in his eyes. "Just…wow."

"*That's* what I was trying to say," Keri said. "You were so much more eloquent."

Kincaid actually laughed. Joe studied him, speculating. Was his plan working? Had Kincaid asked Dixie out yet? She let him carry the container of cranberry sauce, but turned down Joe. What did that mean?

"There are five turkeys," Kincaid said. "Three roasted, one deep fried and one barbecued. There are four kinds of stuffing."

"Four?" Jake looked shocked. "That's not enough variety. What's wrong with this family? We're slipping."

Keri shoved him, laughing.

"Did you see the desserts?" Kincaid went on, still obviously amazed. "I counted twelve pies, and I heard there's more in the garage, where it's cooler. Can you even move after you eat?"

"Sure. We play touch football," Donovan said. "And dodgeball. And whatever else keeps the kids occupied while the dishes are cleaned up."

"Then there's the biggest game of all—take down the tables and chairs," Jake said.

Joe felt his brothers watching him, probably wondering why he wasn't contributing to the conversation. He didn't like how easily Kincaid fit. He and Donovan had graduated from high school together. Most recently, Donovan had rented one of Kincaid's houses. But Kincaid hadn't come to the town picnics and parades, or any other occasion, not that Joe could recall, anyway.

And now he fit in, without awkwardness, without hesitation.

Dixie came out the back door. She stopped for a moment, watching the group, then joined them, coming up next to Kincaid, who smiled at her.

Joe wanted to smash his teeth out.

His fists clenched. He swigged his beer.

"I've got some paperwork for you to sign," Kincaid said to Joe.

"Dixie told me."

Joe felt everyone's gaze on him, and made himself

relax his tone, even as his gut churned. "I can come to your office tomorrow, if you want. How about nine o'clock?"

"That's good. Then I'll stop by your house later and put up the For Sale sign."

Joe looked at his watch. He had to get away before he said or did something regrettable, or even irreparable. "I'm going to help carve a turkey or two."

A little later, dinner was finally served. Joe took a seat at the kids' table, his usual, chosen spot. After a minute, he felt someone sit beside him. Out of the corner of his eye, he caught a flash of golden hair—

"If your family gets any larger, you'll have to start renting a hall," Shana said.

Disappointment hit him hard. He didn't want to examine why.

"If it was only family, Shana, it wouldn't be a problem," he said, then was annoyed at himself. He'd always liked that they opened their home up to others. It was what made the holidays special to him.

"Gee. Thanks so much for making a girl feel welcome." She grabbed her plate and started to stand.

He stopped her. "I'm sorry. I didn't mean you." He'd meant Kincaid, but Joe had no right to complain, since he'd asked his mother to invite the man. "You're family."

She stared at him. "Am not."

"Well, Dixie is. And you're her family. Therefore…"

Shana sat again. "You live in some fantasy world. Just like the rest of your family."

"What's that supposed to mean?"

"You're a smart guy. You figure it out." She took a bite of mashed potatoes and gravy, then closed her eyes. "Oh, man, this is good."

"Uncle Joe. Uncle Joe."

"What, Ethan?" Joe asked the five-year-old seated next to him.

"How come there's no lemon pie? There's always lemon pie. It's your favorite." He grinned. "And mine."

No lemon pie? Dixie hadn't made one? She always made one so that he would have the dessert he loved most.

"Dixie didn't have time, Ethan," Shana said around Joe. "She's been very busy."

"Oh. Do you think if I ask her, she'd make one for me later when she's not busy?"

"I'll tell you what," Shana said. "I'll make you one. We need to let Dixie get her work done for now."

"Okay!"

Shana jabbed her elbow into Joe's side. "Quit moping. It's unmanly."

She had a point. Everything that was happening was because of his own actions. He had no one else to blame. "Men don't mope. They brood," he said.

She laughed. "Brooding only works for Heathcliff and other gothic heroes."

He smiled. "Dix cut your hair."

She shook her head back, her hair soft and healthy, far different from not even a week ago when she'd arrived. "Yeah. Looks nice, hmm? You should try it sometime."

Actually, he'd been thinking about it. Maybe it was

time to look more professional when he made his presentations. Then again, maybe people saw him as a man of the earth, the eco-friendly landscaper, and cutting it might change his image too much.

Regardless, he couldn't ask Dixie to be the one to cut it.

Shana leaned close. "Do you like that guy Kincaid? Do you trust him?"

Everything in Joe went on alert. "Don't you?"

"There's something I can't put my finger on. Dixie says that no one really knows him. That he's lived here for years, but doesn't have friends."

"I think that's overstating it. Maybe he just doesn't have a lot of friends here in town." But she'd identified a problem that made Joe suspicious now, when he hadn't been before. Jealous, yes. He'd been jealous—and angry at himself for setting up a business deal that kept Kincaid and Dixie in close touch.

He should've checked Kincaid out better. There had to be a reason why the man was never seen socializing.

What had started as Joe's way of making it easier on himself to leave had just gotten complicated. Would he now have to keep a closer eye on Dixie instead of moving away from her?

She's a big girl. She can take care of herself.

True. It was just that he was so used to watching over her. It was hard to change a behavior that deeply ingrained.

"So," Joe said to Shana, changing the subject. "How is it being home?"

"I hate living in my parents' house. Hate it. It's like being a teenager again."

"What are you going to do about it?"

"Well, I have no money, so what do you think I can do about it?"

"You're a smart woman. You figure it out," he said, echoing her earlier statement, but tempering the words with a smile.

"Touché."

He nodded. For a few minutes he savored his meal and the kids at the table, getting into the spirit of the moment, enjoying the way they tried to hide the cranberry sauce on their plates under other food, getting a kick out of how many rolls they could consume.

Joe had purposely planted himself with his back to the table where Dixie and Kincaid sat, but he never stopped being aware they were next to each other. Dixie used to sit at the kids' table with Joe.

"What's your work history?" he asked Shana. She'd left for a minute to get Emma, who'd awakened from her nap, crying, and who now gulped down a bottle.

"Waited tables, telemarketing, cleaned cages at a zoo and fed the animals." She gave him a cocky grin. "That job prepared me well for this day."

He laughed. "Do you like being outdoors? Do you mind physical labor?"

"Yes. No."

"I could use some temporary help. My Christmas tree farm opens for the season tomorrow. I'm always looking for good help. Most of my staff are high school and college students, and they end up with surprise projects or performances or mental-health days. Would you be willing to fill in?"

"What about Emma?"

"Look around. Starting with my mom and working down the tables, you've got at least ten willing volunteers."

"I don't know how I can afford to pay for sitting. No offense, Joe, but I don't imagine the job pays a whole lot."

"Hey, Mom!" Joe hollered over the din to his mother at the next table. "How much would you charge to watch Emma if Shana works a few hours a day at the tree farm?"

Shana hissed at Joe. "Stop. Are you out of your—"

"Charge?" Aggie shouted back. "Don't you mean, how much would she charge *me* to watch that adorable peanut?"

"Settled?" he asked Shana.

She nodded once, then touched her forehead to her baby's. "We've never been apart."

"It'll be good for her, too, you know. It takes a village, and all that."

"I know. It's just hard."

"It won't be enough money for you to get a place of your own, but it'll be spending money," he said. "You won't be beholden to your sister."

"She's letting me work it off. I clean the beauty shop and her apartment. She picked up some used furniture, and I'm refinishing it. We're working it out."

"What happens when your parents come home?"

"I don't know. I hadn't planned on staying that long." She leaned close. "I don't want to see them, Joe. Not now. Not ever."

"If you stay, you won't be able to avoid them."

"I know." She looked around, then whispered, "Can Emma and I move in with you?"

Chapter Eight

Almost from the moment she'd arrived for Thanksgiving, Dixie had regretted giving in to Aggie's I-won't-take-no-for-an-answer invitation.

She should be working. The problem was, *everyone* was taking the day off.

As they should.

Right. It was Thanksgiving, after all, she reminded herself—again. However, there was so much to do, and so few hours in a day.

But that wasn't all. She wanted to escape—from Kincaid's attention, from everyone's gazes shifting from her to Joe, looking curious, or worse, sympathetic. Then there was that intense conversation going on between her sister and Joe during most of the meal. What was that about?

Dixie knew neither would confide in her what they'd said, and she had no right to ask. Apparently, however, Shana had lined up a job, which was good.

"Are you still eating or can I take your plate?" Kincaid asked.

She'd eaten about half. "I'm done, thanks. But you don't have to do that."

"Earning my keep. Plus, I need to move around. My stomach is threatening to go on strike." He bent close to her. "Then maybe we could go for a walk and you can tell me why I seem to be getting on your nerves."

Startled, she stared at the table for a few seconds, then watched him disappear into the kitchen. She had no intention of getting that personal with Kincaid, even though he was right. He *had* gotten on her nerves, although she couldn't identify specifically why. All she knew for sure was that he was her landlord and Realtor, and she knew better than to mix business and pleasure.

Her cell phone vibrated in her pocket. She glanced at the screen, saw it was an unknown caller and debated whether to answer. She did, finally, stepping into the front yard, away from the hubbub.

"Hi, sweetheart! Happy Thanksgiving."

"Mom." Dixie looked around as she walked up the street a ways, keeping an eye out for Shana. "Same to you. Where are you?"

"Are you ready for this? Las Vegas!"

They'd been headed for San Diego.

"How'd you end up there?"

"We got lost." Bea laughed.

"But I programmed the GPS system for you. All you had to do was push a button and follow the directions."

"It was too confusing. She kept saying she was re-calculating *all the time*. It drove us both crazy. Get this! Dad won nine hundred dollars playing a slot machine last night. I don't think he's ever going to leave. But it gets better. The National Hardware Show will be held here next week. Can you believe it?"

Dixie laughed. Her parents had owned a hardware store for fifty years and had never gone to a convention. What were the odds of them coming across it out of the blue?

"So, how is Thanksgiving in Vegas?"

"Why, it's amazing. The abundance of food? My word. And everyone is so nice and friendly. It's not as good as dinner at Aggie's, of course, but I didn't have to fix it. Or clean up." She sounded happy and relaxed.

"How's Dad? Is he managing the RV okay?"

"Perfect. We couldn't have done it without you, Dixie. You're the best daughter ever. Everything is okay there, right?"

Dixie had thought she might test the waters about Shana when her parents checked in, and tell them she'd heard from their long-lost daughter. But hearing how happy her mother was, she decided not to—although she knew it might come back to bite her at some point.

"Everything is fine, Mom. Don't worry about anything. Sales are holding steady. Doug's doing a great job. Everyone asks about you and hopes you're enjoying yourselves."

"Tell them yes! I don't suppose you went to Aggie's this year."

"Actually, I did. Aggie insisted."

"That woman. Honestly."

"Please don't, Mom." Dixie may be wishing she hadn't come to dinner today, but she wouldn't stand for any criticism of Aggie McCoy, who'd loved her unconditionally, who'd mothered her in ways her own mother hadn't. "What's your plan for after the hardware show?"

"We don't know. What do you think about that? We're having the best time, Dixie. He's eating again," she said soft and low.

"Why wasn't he before?"

"I think he's been depressed. I saw a show about it on Oprah." Her voice picked up again. "I've got to go now. Dad's waving me over. We've got reservations for some fancy show or other. Give everyone my best."

Feeling herself grinning, Dixie shoved her phone in her pocket. She had never heard her mother so excited about anything. Ever.

"You didn't tell them about me," Shana said from behind her. "Thanks."

Dixie turned around. "It wasn't the right time. And I'm thinking you should be the one to do the telling. I'm done with being the mediator in this family."

"Fair enough. I gather I have a few more days?"

Dixie reached for Emma, who giggled and stuck her fingers in Dixie's mouth. "Looks like they're staying through next week, anyway."

"A lot can happen in a week," she said in a tone that made Dixie wonder. Shana kept so much to herself.

"So, you're going to work for Joe." They headed back to the house. There was still cleanup to do and dessert to be served.

"Can't turn down anything that pays, can I? I'm not qualified in any traditional ways for a lot of jobs. But I work hard and, believe it or not, I'm always on time." She put her hands behind her back and looked straight ahead. "I asked Joe if I could live at his house. Your house. Whatever you call it. I mean, he says he's going to be gone a lot, and so it's just sitting there. But he said no. That it wouldn't look right."

Relief blanketed Dixie before she knew how she even felt about the situation. "You hate living at Mom and Dad's that much?"

"I can't begin to tell you. I don't have a single good memory from that place, Dix. Not one." She grabbed her daughter's hand and kissed it. "If it weren't for Emma, I'd just as soon sleep in my car."

"If it weren't for Emma, you wouldn't even be in Chance City."

Shana shrugged. "Moot point, I guess."

They walked into the house. Dixie spotted Joe first, then Kincaid just beyond him. Feeling stuck, she sent a smile toward both of them, passed Emma to Shana, then took off for the kitchen to hide.

Behind her, Shana clucked softly.

Dixie started to turn around, annoyed. Then she laughed. As complicated as her life had gotten, keeping her sense of humor was a priority.

Even if it was at her own expense.

"That was quite an event yesterday," Kincaid said the next morning, inviting Joe to take a seat across from his. His large mahogany desk was free of clutter, only one file folder on the desktop. His office was small, with no assistant, or even a place for one.

Joe found himself looking for reasons to mistrust the man now that Shana had planted that seed. "Some years are wilder than others."

"How would you rank yesterday's?"

Joe thought it over. "Somewhere in the middle. There were more people than usual, but better behavior. Most of my nieces and nephews are in their twenties now and not as rowdy as they were, but they also brought dates."

"Is your Christmas like that?"

"Mom usually has an open house from noon on, so people come and go." He couldn't tell if Kincaid was cringing at the thought or just curious. "You get used to it."

"If you say so." He opened the single folder and placed the paperwork in front of Joe. "Look these over, then sign where I've put the flags."

Having never sold property before, Joe took his time reviewing the papers. Kincaid didn't drum his fingers on the desktop, but he did a certain amount of shifting around. So. He wasn't as patient as he seemed.

"Do you have any questions?" Kincaid asked, looking at his watch.

"Am I keeping you from something?"

He hesitated. "I've got a haircut at nine-thirty."

With Dixie. The unspoken words loomed large.

"I could come back." *Anything to stall the deal.* That realization struck hard. He didn't want to sign the papers, didn't want to set the sale in motion now that he had doubts about Kincaid. He'd been so sure before….

He stacked the papers. "I'll just take them with me to look over. Have my lawyer take a look." His lawyer would have to be his newest sister-in-law, since she was the only lawyer he knew, although she did family law, not real estate.

Joe stood before Kincaid could argue the point, but a speculative look settled in Kincaid's eyes, as if he knew what Joe was up to, had recognized the stall for what it was.

"Maybe you'd prefer to list with another Realtor," Kincaid said, following Joe to the door. "Someone you feel more comfortable with."

What are your intentions regarding Dixie? Joe wanted to ask, even though he'd help set that ball in motion.

"I've never sold a house before," Joe said, instead of

the question shouting in his head. "I like to know what I'm getting myself into."

Kincaid nodded. "Okay. Give me a call when you're ready."

Joe noticed the For Sale sign leaning against the wall by the door then. He hadn't seen it when he'd come into the office because his back had been to it. The reality struck him hard. He didn't want to give up his house. Even without Dixie.

He wanted a place to come home to, a house that was his, not a rented apartment or whatever other home base he'd thought he would have.

Joe extended a hand to Kincaid. "I'll be in touch."

Laura's office was two doors down from Dixie's beauty shop, so he ended up following Kincaid and seeing him enter the shop as Joe walked from his truck into Laura's office. Neither man acknowledged the other.

"Why, if it isn't Joseph McCoy himself." Dolly Bannister, Laura's sociable mother and assistant, manned the lobby desk. "I didn't get a chance to hug you yesterday in that mass of humanity." She did so then.

Laura came out of her private office, looking as cool and collected as any beauty-queen-turned-lawyer ever was. She'd learned to let her hair down lately, since Donovan and Ethan had become part of her life. Joe's brother and nephew had been good for her—and vice versa.

"Got a minute?" Joe asked Laura.

She gestured toward her office. "You'll be rescuing me from a mound of paperwork."

"Which she needs to get done," Dolly said. "That's what you get for going on a honeymoon."

Laura shut the door. "We've been back a week, and I'm still trying to get out from under it all. Have a seat, Joe. You look a little shell-shocked."

Which was exactly how he felt. "This is a contract for the sale of my house. I'm sure it's standard, but I'd like you to read it."

"I'd be happy to."

"And find something in it that will let me stall."

She sat back, her eyes searching his. "Talk to me, Joe."

"If I could put it into words, I would. I just realized I was making a mistake, but I have to think it through, beginning to end, before I do anything about it."

"Well, I *am* deep in paperwork at the moment. It would be easy for me to put off looking at it for, say, a week. Is that long enough?"

"For the moment. Dixie's loan for her shop is secured, regardless of the house sale, so there's no reason for me to rush because of that. She's okay."

"It may not affect her financially, but personally she'll wonder."

He couldn't talk to Shana about Dixie, but could he ask Laura, one of Dixie's best friends, *Is she dating Kincaid?* It was a simple question—

That he couldn't ask. Had no right to ask. "I can't explain it."

"Can't or won't? I'm now your lawyer, Joe, and your sister-in-law. I'll keep your confidences."

"You're one of Dixie's best friends, too."

Her brows arched high. "Ah. I see. Having a change of heart, are you?"

He waited a beat, letting the question settle. "About the house, yes."

She smiled, that kind of secretive smile that women used when they'd known something you didn't know yourself, then it turned out they were right. He knew that smile well. He'd been surrounded by women all his life.

"Okay, Joe. I'll take a week looking over your contract. You let me know if you want me to take less or more time. But let me tell you this much about Kincaid—when he sees something he wants, he goes after it, and I'm not just talking about property."

"I figured that out. But thanks."

Joe resisted the temptation to walk past Dixie's shop. He drove to his Christmas tree farm instead. Shana was there, learning the ropes.

"I didn't know so many people chose their Christmas tree the day after Thanksgiving," she said.

"Tradition. Can't mess with it."

"The trees smell so good." She walked with him as he went up and down the rows, assuring himself that everything was in order. "Almost puts me in the mood for Christmas."

"Do you think you'll be here?"

She shrugged.

"How was it leaving Emma at Mom's?"

"I cried all the way here." She gave Joe an isn't-that-ridiculous look. "And another part of me is happy to get a breather. I couldn't plunge into a full-time job yet, I don't think, but this is okay. Thank you."

"Glad I could help."

"Kincaid walked her home last night," she said without preamble.

Joe was beginning to wonder about Shana's motives for continuing to bring up Kincaid. Was she really worried that he wasn't what he seemed and therefore might present a danger to Dixie? Or was Shana trying to make him jealous? Maybe it was payback because he hadn't let her live at his house.

Whatever her reason, he wasn't going to play the game.

"Okay," he said, even though it bothered the hell out of him that Kincaid had walked Dixie home. Had he given her a hug? Kissed her good-night?

"Okay? That's it?"

"That's it." He'd do his own investigating, make up his own mind. "Now. Let's pick out a tree for Nana Mae and put a Sold sign on it. She won't want it for a couple more weeks."

Shana walked silently beside him as he looked at trees. Nana Mae liked hers to touch the ceiling, which meant a ten-footer. He found the perfect tree and tied a Sold sign to it. Only then did he look at Shana—and noted the furrow between her brows and her set mouth.

"You have something to say?" he asked.

"Yes, I do." She leaned close as a customer came into view. "Maybe you've washed your hands of my sister, but I haven't. She's already driving herself crazy with the amount of work she's taken on, so she's vulnerable, you know? A man who can relieve some of her burdens stands a good chance with her right now."

"She broke up with me a year ago."

"That's no reason not to care what happens to her."

"I care," he said angrily. He cared too much, in fact, and he was taking care of it, of her.

"Then act like it. Life's short, Joe. Way too short." She marched off.

She threw her head back and forced a smile as she approached the wandering customer.

He was supposed to leave town again on Sunday and be gone for at least a week, his first trip out of state, to Portland, Oregon. Several small towns in the area had come together as a group, looking for ways to be kinder to their landscape, to get people involved in doing more for the environment.

If this was a success, his world could open up beyond his expectations.

But first he had to know that Dixie would be all right.

He waited until it was dark, until he knew the downtown shops would be closing. Then he made his way to Dixie's salon.

From across the street, he watched her through the window as she talked with his niece Caroline and Nana Mae, both of whom looked like they'd just had their hair done. Joe stayed in the shadows until they left, out the back door to the parking lot.

Dixie grabbed a broom and swept around her chair.

Joe opened the door.

She looked up, smiling, then went still. After a moment she straightened, leaning on the broom. "Is everything okay?"

"I need a haircut. I was hoping you'd do it."

Chapter Nine

Dixie ignored the flash of heat that zapped her. Seeing him framed in the doorway, looking so familiar and yet…*not,* shook her up.

She was afraid to be alone with him. Afraid to touch him, which she would have to do, in order to cut his hair.

She grabbed the long-handled dustpan and swept the hair from Caroline's cut into it. "Your mom always trims your hair for you."

"I don't want a trim. I want it cut short. Professional."

Her mouth had to be hanging open. "Seriously?" He'd grown his hair long when he was fourteen, had kept it shoulder length, but always pulled back.

"Yeah. It's time, don't you think? Will you do it?"

"There's another salon in town. Plus Ernie's barber-shop."

"I'm aware of that." He locked the door behind him and closed the blinds. "No one will know. I don't trust anyone but you."

"You shut the blinds." What did that mean?

"For your sake, Dix. I don't think you'd want to broadcast this."

"I haven't said I would do it."

He smiled. "You will. You know why?"

"I'm sure you're going to tell me."

"Because you wouldn't trust anyone else to do it right. You've already got a picture in your head of what kind of cut I should have, and no one else will duplicate that."

He hadn't come any closer, and she knew he would take no for an answer. But he was so right about his hair. She didn't want anyone else to be the one to give him a style all his own.

An even more important issue loomed, however. She didn't think he just wanted to look more professional. This was his way of starting his new life. Of getting rid of the weight of the old life.

She could do that for him, wanted to help him start down that road.

"Where'd you park?" she asked.

"I walked."

"You just missed your grandmother and niece."

"I know. I waited." He still hadn't moved and stood very still, his arms crossed, but otherwise not looking defensive.

She turned and walked to her station. "Well, come on, then."

He sat in the chair. She wrapped a towel around his neck, then a soft plastic cape.

"When will work start on the place?" he asked, looking around.

Nothing had changed yet. There were four stations, three dryers, three sinks and a reception desk, plus a rack of products for sale, but there was unused space, too, where she would expand.

"On Monday, I hope. The mobile salon is being delivered then, and Bruno's supposed to start the demo." She'd been cutting hair for years, had always been good at it, and was even better now with professional training, but she was scared to cut his hair. What if she goofed? Would he think she'd done it on purpose? She didn't want to get into an argument with him. She was stressed enough already.

She considered options for his cut. Go short and stylish, something popular with guys his age today? Or a slightly longer businessman's look? Or maybe a little longer than that, so that the transition after all these years would be easier for him?

She decided to take it short. He was only thirty, and his field was one in which people often wore Earth shoes and linen. He didn't do that, but he could look current.

"I'll do an initial cut first. Get rid of most of the length. There's enough to donate, okay?" she asked, scissors in hand.

"Yeah."

"Would you rather not face the mirror?"

He smiled slightly. "Would you call me a coward?"

"Never in a hundred years, Joe."

The air crackled around them. She'd known it was a mistake for them to be alone, had known the tension would be unbearable. Add to that the fact she had to touch him, to run her fingers through his hair, which brought back a thousand memories—

"Then I'd rather not watch," he said.

She made the first snip above the band. "No turning back now."

"Just get it over with."

He flinched with every cut. So did she. Nerves, she told herself. Just nerves. It was a lot of pressure cutting his hair.

Liar. The pressure came mostly from being this close, touching him, knowing he probably felt the same tension. Finally she laid aside the bundle of hair, not holding it for him to see. She took up the scissors again and worked methodically, precisely, her nerves sizzling, hands shaking.

He pointedly looked at them, then at her face.

"Harder than I thought," she said.

"For me, too." He took her hands in his, the point of the scissors dangerously close to his heart. "But not just because of my hair."

"Me, too," she whispered. He already looked so different, he could be someone else altogether.

"You haven't cut off my strength, have you?" he asked, his eyes twinkling just a little, the Joe she remembered.

"I'm not channeling Delilah, Samson." She tried to smile back at him, but his hands tightened on hers, feeling warm and comfortable…and exciting. She felt her nipples tighten, saw him notice. "Let's go to the shampoo bowl."

She turned on the water, let it heat up. "Tell me if the water temperature is comfortable."

"It feels good," he said, closing his eyes.

She pumped shampoo into her palm and lathered his hair, taking her time. She glanced at his face, at his long, thick eyelashes that she'd often wished she had. Why did so many men have such gorgeous, long lashes, anyway?

Dixie shampooed his hair much longer than she did anyone else's, enjoying the task, remembering the many times she'd washed his hair, and he had washed hers. And each other's bodies. She recalled vividly how he felt under her soapy hands. They'd always ended up in bed after taking a shower together. Always.

"Are you okay?" he asked now, taking her out of the memory.

"Fine." She wasn't, of course, but neither was he. He'd started off relaxed. Now he wasn't. She didn't have to look at him to know, but she did, catching him looking at her, or rather, her breasts, which were in his direct line of vision.

Dixie wasn't wearing anything she considered sexy, just a sage-green T-shirt with three-quarter sleeves—

although it did hug her curves, which were more generous than average, something he'd always appreciated.

"Did you take this long shampooing Kincaid's hair?" he asked, his voice taut.

"His hair is much shorter."

Their gazes met. He waited in silence. She knew her answer mattered to him, and recognized something had shifted between them.

"No," she said finally, softly. "I didn't."

He closed his eyes again and relaxed, but she didn't linger. She rinsed his hair and had him move to her chair again. Before she started cutting, she turned up the volume on the music playing through the speakers, tunes shuffling on her iPod.

"Don't want to talk to me?" he asked as she combed his wet hair, his back still to the mirror.

She would. She just needed a minute, then she would keep the conversation focused on safe topics. Although nothing seemed safe at the moment.

She was completely aware of him. Of his tension, his awareness of her, even his breathing. She wanted to touch more than his hair. She wanted to climb into his chair, straddle his lap, kiss him. Oh, yeah, she wanted to kiss him, to feel the heat and wetness of his mouth.

She dropped her scissors onto the floor, took a step back, afraid to continue, afraid she would ruin his hair.

"Done?" he asked.

She shook her head. "Not quite. I don't want to mess up."

"You won't." He ran his hands over his hair, then swallowed. "Short."

His seeming acceptance steadied her. "It'll look good. It already does," she said. She picked up the scissors, traded them for a fresh pair, and started again, then used the clippers. A few minutes later she was done. She ran some gel through his hair, then played with it until she was satisfied with the look.

"Ready to see?" she asked, dragging the drape off him.

"Yes."

She turned his chair. She waited for his reaction, but he didn't say anything, just stared at his image, his hands folded in his lap. "It'll take you a little while to get used to it," she said, nerves making the words come out shaky. "Your neck will feel cold, too."

His continued silence made her heart thump.

"Really, Joe, give it a few—"

"I like it."

She almost deflated with relief. "I'll give you some gel. You'll need it if you want it to stand up like that in the front."

"I feel up-to-date."

"That was the point." She grabbed the broom and started sweeping the floor around him. "And please don't ask how much you owe me. It's a gift."

She just wanted him to leave, before it was too late. Every cell, every nerve ending, every hormone was dancing inside her, dizzying and reckless.

"Dix."

It was his tone that did her in. He'd uttered one syllable, yet she heard need and desire and even a little desperation—everything she felt, too.

She finally looked him, at his tight jaw, hungry eyes, appealing mouth.

She dropped the broom, the stick clattering. Music filled the air, no lyrics, just a sultry sound. She started to move forward, then stopped. Took a step back, then another.

"You need to go," she said, wishing otherwise, but knowing it would be a big mistake.

"Dixie—"

"I mean it, Joe." She closed her eyes for a moment, trying to center her thoughts. "Look, I haven't been with anyone else. I haven't even touched anyone else. That makes me extremely vulnerable right now, because you're familiar. And safe. But not emotionally. I can't do it."

"I haven't been with anyone, either." He got out of the chair and came toward her.

She didn't question his honesty, and the truth of it tempted her in ways that stunned her. "You need to go," she repeated. "Really. Right now."

They stood facing each other like duelists, their weapons invisible, internal.

He reached for her. She had no fight in her. It was what she wanted.

Then his lips touched hers and everything spun. His lips, his tongue, the scent of his skin aroused her, excited her. His arms came around her, strong and steady, until they were body to body, and she could feel him shaking, too.

"Dixie," he breathed. "Dixie."

She'd been living for this moment, and now was dying in it. All they had to do was go upstairs. She would be happy again. He was everything—

A knock sounded. "Dix? Are you there?"

Shana. Dixie shoved away from him.

"Dix? I know you're there. I hear music. It's cold out here!"

"Go out the front door," Dixie urged him.

He pointed to his head. "Thanks."

She came out of her stupor when he opened the door. "Hang on." She grabbed a tube of hair gel and tossed it to him.

He caught it on the fly, shoved it in his back pocket.

Dixie waited for the door to shut then went to the back door and let Shana and Emma in.

"What took you so long?" Shana asked.

"I'd gone upstairs to get…something." She grabbed the broom and started sweeping up.

"You worked late," Shana said, coming closer.

"Sometimes I have to, you know. For people who work out of town."

Shana picked up Joe's ponytail, dangled it from her fingers. "Or someone who wants a confidential appointment."

Dixie looked at the floor, then she carefully took the

bundle away from her sister. "Keep it to yourself, please. He wanted it done and wouldn't trust anyone else."

Shana zipped her lips.

"If you'd like to be helpful, I could use another hand or two helping me set up for Bitty's farewell party tomorrow. A lot of people will be in and out all day to say goodbye. I'd like this place to sparkle, plus I've got decorations to hang and cookies to bake, although I made the dough last night. What would you like to tackle?"

"Let's work together. The time will fly by. But please, can we turn on some different music? This stuff is going to put me to sleep."

Dixie smiled. "That's salon music." She tapped the screen on her iPod until she found the Black Eyed Peas playlist.

The sisters danced while they decorated, singing loudly, although not exactly on key. Shana suggested Dixie put up a poster of the renovation plans to start drumming up business for the spa services.

An hour later the salon was ready. Soon after, the scent of oatmeal cookies filled Dixie's apartment. She gave Emma a bottle while Shana baked, offering to take over.

Emma fell asleep in Dixie's arms. She'd borrowed the porta-crib from Joe, so Emma would have a place to sleep other than in her carrier, but for now Dixie put the baby on her shoulder and rubbed her back as she walked up to the breakfast bar and watched Shana heap dough onto a cookie sheet.

"Last batch," she said. "Emma adores you."

"It's mutual."

"Is the clock ticking for you, Dix?"

"I don't feel desperate yet, but I don't want to wait until I'm almost forty, like Mom was. How'd the job go today?" Dixie asked, changing the subject. She bounced a little as Emma stirred.

"It was fun. I saw a lot of people I remember. Guess it's a good thing that Mom and Dad aren't checking in with friends and neighbors or they would've been home by now."

"I think you're right."

"You'll be in trouble for not telling them, won't you? And especially for letting me stay at the house."

"They'll get over it." Eventually. "If they want to keep on RV-ing, they need me. Leverage? It's priceless." Dixie wiggled her brows, making Shana laugh.

"Maybe Emma will be my leverage. She is their only grandchild." She slid the tray of cookies into the oven and set the timer, then passed Dixie a cooled cookie from an earlier batch, taking one for herself.

If their parents had been the nurturing kind, Dixie might agree with her sister. "I guess that means you plan to stay for a while."

Shana shrugged. "No place better to go."

Dixie didn't buy it. Shana had come home for a reason. She just wasn't sharing that reason yet. "Does Emma have other grandparents?"

Shana bit off a piece of cookie and stared at Dixie as she chewed. "Yes," she said finally.

"Yet you didn't go to them. Even knowing Mom and Dad wouldn't welcome you with open arms, you didn't go to anyone else."

"I came to you. And Joe, or so I thought, not knowing about your split. Or maybe that's not the case anymore?"

"Nothing's changed, Shana." Which was a lie. She'd been numb for a year. Now everything in her and around her crackled with energy.

Shana took Emma when her fussing increased, swaddled her, then sat in the rocking chair that had been moved from Joe's house. "I still can't believe you let him go. You even said you still love him."

"It isn't enough." She had to remind herself of that a lot these days so that she stayed on track.

"Love is everything, Dixie. Everything." She wasn't looking at Dixie, but at Emma. "I loved her father with all my heart, and I would give anything for one more day with him. We didn't get to say goodbye. I needed to say goodbye. It's like, I don't know, an unfinished symphony."

Dixie sat on the sofa, close to Shana. "Was he—"

"No questions. Please." Her voice quavered. Tears filled her eyes. "I'm just trying to get you to open your eyes. See what's in front of you. *Who* is in front of you. You should be doing everything you can to keep him. Or you should tell him goodbye and move on."

"I've already moved on. So has he."

"No, you haven't. If you had, you would be dating, and seeing him wouldn't be so obviously painful to you. You wouldn't have cut his hair for him—or looked so guilty when I came in."

Shana gave Dixie one long look, then stood. "I need to get the munchkin home. The car ride will soothe her, and I'm ready for bed, too."

The timer went off. Dixie went into the kitchen and pulled out the cookie sheet. "Thank you for all your help. I really do appreciate it."

Shana settled Emma in her carrier. "You know, Dix. You are the worst person on the planet when it comes to asking for help. Plenty of us would pitch in, but first we have to know you need us to. Nobody likes a martyr."

Dixie didn't know whether to be angry. *Had* she become that stridently independent, not accepting help that people genuinely wanted to give?

She followed her sister downstairs then out to her car, locking Emma's carrier into the base while Shana started the car to let it heat up. Dixie shut the door to the backseat.

"Thanks again," she said.

Shana got out of the car and hugged Dixie. Neither of them spoke.

Dixie stood shivering as they drove off. She went back upstairs, turned on the bathwater, added some liquid bubble bath, then slipped into the frothy water, where she did some of her best thinking.

Thanks to Shana, she had plenty to think about.

Chapter Ten

Another Saturday night at the Stompin' Grounds. Joe sat in his truck, hesitant to go inside. He'd been kidded and complimented about his haircut all day, so he knew there would be more of that ahead.

He wasn't in the mood. He should be home packing for his week in Portland. Plus, he wasn't sure he wanted to see Dixie, not after last night.

She hadn't been off his mind for a second, had barely slept, and when he did, he'd dreamed about her. Too much unfinished business.

"I haven't been with anyone else," she'd said. He was glad, even as he knew it signaled something deeper— that she hadn't moved on with her life.

He could say the same thing of himself, of course, except that in other ways, he was moving on. And now that he was traveling beyond Chance City, he knew he would be tempted by everything new, even other women.

At least that's what Jake and Donovan said.

First he had to get over the fact it would feel like he was cheating on Dixie. Maybe she was feeling the same.

Joe walked across the parking lot. Dixie's car wasn't in sight, but he was earlier than usual. Maybe she would come, see his truck and leave. He didn't know how she felt about what had happened between them last night.

"Hey, McCoy," someone called when the door shut behind him. "Who scalped you, man?"

Joe grinned, ignoring the rest of the comments shouted out, his favorite from Max Bailey. "It's about time you stopped lookin' like a girl!"

Bubba Krakauer got up from his stool then, all six-feet-five, two hundred and eighty pounds of him, his fists clenched and his ponytail quivering. "You sayin' I look like a girl, Maxwell?"

The short, lanky Max shook his head. "Nope. Sure ain't. Not me, Bubba. Hey, barkeep, give Bubba a cold one on me, okay?"

Bubba stared Max down.

"Well, all right, a pitcher then," Max said. "And a draft for my friend Joe there."

Everyone laughed, Bubba nodded and peace was restored.

A mug came sliding down the bar. Joe caught it, then saluted Max with it.

"Evening, Joe." Kincaid took the stool next to Joe and signaled an order to the bartender.

"Kincaid." The last person Joe wanted to see. He didn't want to watch him hanging around Dixie. Joe didn't want to run off again, either. This was *his* bar on Saturday. Kincaid was the intruder.

"How's the paperwork coming?" Kincaid asked.

"I can't get it back to you for at least a week. I'm leaving town."

Kincaid took a thoughtful sip, then set his mug down quietly. "You sure you want to sell, Joe?"

"I'm the one who approached you, remember?" Joe wasn't about to confide in the man.

Kincaid held up both hands. "Fine." After a couple of seconds, he said, "Nice haircut."

"Thanks." Unfortunately, it was too early for the band, and although the jukebox was turned up, it wasn't loud enough to make conversation impossible.

"Dixie's an artist," Kincaid said, lifting his mug, eyeing Joe over the rim. "Don't bother to deny it. I saw you go into the shop last night. Saw you shut the blinds."

Fire flared in Joe's stomach. For himself he didn't care that Kincaid knew, but he did care for Dixie. "Didn't know you were a voyeur, Kincaid."

He waited a few beats. "That wasn't my intention. Wrong time, wrong place."

"And none of your business."

"Well, now, Joe, that's where you're wrong. Dixie's become a friend. She's got a goal, and I'm interested in helping her get there."

Joe tamped down his jealousy to appreciate the man's honesty and integrity, although Joe wasn't entirely convinced that Kincaid wasn't interested in Dixie in ways far beyond friendship and concern for her success. But Joe gave the man more of an answer than he'd given to anyone else, including his family. "I wanted my hair cut. I knew Dixie would do the best job. I closed the blinds to protect her from gossip. If you were watching, then you know I wasn't there long."

"I didn't hang around."

Joe's cell phone rang. He looked at the screen. Dixie? Really? "I need to get this," he said to Kincaid, then headed out of the bar. "Hey," he said, feeling as if he'd conjured her up by thinking about her so much, talking about her.

"Are you at the Stompin' Grounds?"

"Yeah. How come you aren't?" It'd crossed his mind that she might avoid him.

"I decided to stay home. It was a very long day."

He reached the parking lot, no longer had to struggle to hear her. "So, what's up?"

"Kincaid told me that you haven't signed the paperwork."

"That's right."

"Why not?"

"I took the contract to Laura. She's looking at it for me, but she's been swamped since she got back from her honeymoon, and I'm leaving town tomorrow for a week, so…"

"You're leaving for a week?"

"Yeah. Portland."

"Joe?"

Her tone put him on alert. "What?"

"We never said goodbye."

He frowned. "Shana showed up. You told me to leave. I left. I figured that—"

"Not last night," she interrupted. "You and I talk about things being over between us, and we're selling the house, but we let the relationship just drift to an end. We've never said goodbye."

"What's the purpose of saying goodbye, if we'll see each other again? It's not like I'm leaving the country."

He heard her blow out a long breath, which usually preceded her saying something crucial that she wished she didn't have to say.

"This is important, Joe. I need this. I think you do, too. We need to say goodbye, so that it'll end. I didn't sleep at all last night."

"Join the club." But he tested the idea in his head. Maybe she was right. Maybe that *was* what they needed. Most people who had been together for as long as they had ended their relationship by getting a divorce. Maybe there needed to be something official for couples who hadn't married. *Them.*

"Do you mean, like, a ceremony of some kind?" he asked.

"Whatever it takes. Something that feels official."

"When?"

"I don't know. Now, maybe? Get it over with."

"Okay." He wanted it to be done, too. That kiss last night lingered in his mind. "I'm on my way."

"I'll leave the back door unlocked. Just come upstairs."

He ended the call as he climbed into his truck then headed to her apartment. He'd almost arrived when he made a U-turn instead. He couldn't leave his truck there. He called her as he started walking from his house, covering the three long blocks in record time. He went through the door from the parking lot, locked it and took her stairs slowly, aware they would be alone. Had to be alone. Maybe it would've been safer to do this in public, but they couldn't.

The door to her apartment stood open. She was curled up on her sofa, wearing her usual Wranglers but with a fuzzy pink sweater and matching socks. She didn't get up, didn't offer him any refreshments.

He sat on the same sofa at arm's length.

"Thank you for coming."

"It's a good idea," he said, wishing he could pull her feet into his lap and rub them like he'd done so many times in the past. It had almost always led to more.

"Any thoughts about what to do next?" she asked.

"I've considered and eliminated several. But the one that got stuck in my head and won't let loose is that I want to finish the kiss from last night."

"It felt finished to me."

He smiled slightly. "I'd barely begun."

She searched his eyes for a long time, then looked away. He gave her time to decide without trying to influence her. Somehow he didn't think most divorces ended with a kiss. But then, this wasn't a divorce. It only felt like one.

"Okay," she said finally, her voice soft but sure, her eyes turning the deepest green he'd ever seen.

He didn't want to kiss her yet, because then he would have to leave, and he didn't want to do that, either. But he didn't see any way around it. They couldn't just sit here and have a normal conversation.

"Do you want to stand?" he asked.

She nodded. He stood, then held out a hand to her, drawing her up, leaving it up to her how much distance should be between them—to start with. She surprised him by getting close enough for her breasts to touch his chest. He sucked in a breath at the sensation, then he cupped her face.

"I remember our first kiss very well, Dix. Do you?"

"Yes."

"It started like this." He barely touched her lips, retreated for a couple of seconds, then returned, pressing his lips to hers a little longer.

"It ended like that, too," she said, her eyes smiling just a little. "We didn't know what else to do."

"We do now." He pulled her closer, sliding one hand low on her back, pressing until their hips touched, then he took the kiss well beyond the simple beginning, involving open mouths and seeking tongues. Her throat vibrated with low sounds of need. Shock waves rolled through him. They'd shared long, hot kisses before, but he couldn't remember one like this. He didn't want it to end. She was going to have to stop it, because he couldn't.

"Joe," she said, pulling her mouth free and leaning her forehead against his throat.

"I'm right here."

"I don't want to stop. I want—" Her breath was hot and shaky. Her fingers gripped his chest.

"What? What do you want?" he asked, hoping.

"You. All of you."

He knew he should give her a minute to think about it, to make sure she wouldn't have regrets, but he couldn't. "How long of a goodbye is this?" he asked instead. "Is this a one-time-then-kick-me-out deal or do we have all night?"

She laughed softly, turning her face so that her head lay against his shoulder. She toyed with his shirt, unsnapping it, her hands brushing his chest as she went.

"Dix, you really need to answer the question. If it's only one time, I have to figure out a way not to put you up against the wall right this second."

"Put me up against the wall."

All night. They were going to have all night.

Instead of making him rush, as his body demanded, the idea that he had all night helped him put the brakes on. He wanted to savor. They had the advantage of knowing each other's needs and desires and arousal points. It could end up being the best sex of their lives....

And then they would say goodbye.

She'd finished unsnapping his shirt and was pulling it free. She pressed her lips to his chest, then used her tongue, leaving cold, wet trails.

He wanted to be skin-to-skin. Needed to. He lifted her into his arms and carried her to bed as she nibbled on his ear, her breath warm, making him shiver. The air smelled of her perfume, subtle and sexy. Candles, he realized, surprised to see some lit.

He set her down next to the bed, peeled her sweater over her head, found a matching pink lacy bra underneath that he got rid of right away. Jeans, socks, underwear all came off. She undressed him then. Her hands felt like fire.

"Don't you want music?" he asked. She loved having music on while they made love, always chose it according to her mood.

"No."

"Why not?"

She hesitated. Finally she said, "I'm afraid one song would stand out. Then every time I heard it, I'd be thinking, you know. About you. About this moment."

They had a song, their song, a Bryan Adams tune that had come out the year they were freshmen. It had been playing on the radio when they'd had their first kiss. It *had* been all for love then, as the song went, and for a long time after.

She tossed her head, her hair dancing. She looked uncomfortable at his silence, but faced him squarely. "So, if you want music, you'll have to sing," she said.

He moved her onto the bed.

"She'll be comin' 'round the mountain when she comes," he sang, low and twangy.

She laughed. "Thank you," she said, as she shoved the bedding out of the way, her glorious body more perfect than he'd remembered.

"My pleasure." There was nothing between them now, not even the pain of the past year. Just the joy of rediscovery, and so much anticipation. Again, he instinctively wanted to ask if she was sure. Was it the right thing to do? He decided to give his instincts the night off. Sometimes need trumped everything else.

Joe curved his hands over her breasts, feeling her nipples press into his palms. He couldn't believe no one else had touched her, was irrationally pleased about it.

He jumped when she touched him then, trailing her fingers down his chest, his stomach, his abdomen… beyond. He clenched his teeth, made a hissing sound, wrapped a hand around her wrist, stopping her explorations. "I wanted to go slow, Dix."

"Not me." She smiled, hot and sultry. "So, just shut up and kiss me."

He found a compromise, pulling her down, stretching out next to her, avoiding her touch by overwhelming her instead, which gave him pleasure beyond belief. He cherished every luscious curve with his hands then let his mouth take over, drawing her nipples into his mouth, feeling her back arch, hearing her moan.

"Please, Joe. Please…" She drew out the word, pulling at his shoulders, trying to get him to move above her.

But if this was goodbye, he wanted her to remember every minute, every touch. He kissed her, not gently, not restrained, their tongues doing battle. She clutched him as he slid his hand down her, encountering her heat, wet and ready. He rose up high enough to watch her face then pressed a fingertip against her. Instantly, she rose up, called his name, dug her fingers into his flesh as she climaxed, loud and long.

He couldn't hold back after that. He settled on top of her, her legs wrapping around him, her hands cupping his face, bringing him down to kiss, openmouthed, demanding. Then he found home, the explosion instantaneous, mutual, infinite, rocketing him to a planet in a faraway galaxy. *Extraordinary,* he thought as he slowly came back to earth. To life. Real life.

Extraordinary.

After he caught his breath, he rolled onto his side, taking her with him, tucking her close. He hoped she didn't want to talk, because he didn't have anything to say. There was too much running through his head, words that made no sense, that defied logic.

She hadn't relaxed against him, either, but clung hard. He didn't want to know what was on her mind, either.

Maybe later, but not now.

He caught the quilt with his foot and dragged it up, then settled it over them. After a couple of long, silent minutes he stopped wishing she wouldn't speak. He wanted to know how she felt.

How does this change things, Dix? Will we be able to see each other from now on and not be either angry or craving, but actually just be friends? Is that even possible?

If he asked those questions, she would answer him honestly. He didn't doubt that.

But while he'd been debating, she'd fallen asleep. He was on the brink himself after his previous sleepless night.

He tried to slide out of the bed without waking her. She grabbed hold of him, made a sound of protest.

"I'm going to blow out the candles," he said against her hair. "I'll be right back."

Twenty seconds later, he climbed in bed and gathered her close.

"You're cold," she said, sleep in her voice.

"Warm me."

She entwined herself with him, sighed deeply, then fell asleep, her body a furnace.

Tangled together, he slept, too.

Chapter Eleven

Dixie caught the scent of him first, then his heart beating against her ear, slow and steady. Soothing. Her wrist was resting on his hip, her fingertips grazing his taut rear. She curved her hand over him, stroked his muscular flesh. His muscles twitched.

He was the same man she'd known her whole life, and yet he wasn't. Physically, the only difference was that she couldn't run her fingers through his hair anymore. But beyond that? She couldn't talk to him the way she used to—openly, honestly, without fear he would misunderstand.

In fact, they'd both changed. The reasons for her transformation were simple. She was compelling herself to be independent, to deal with her contractor without him calling her "little lady," to face financial responsibilities she'd never had. And not to be so dependent on the McCoys to fill so many of the needs in her life.

Then there was Shana, and having to keep her a secret from her parents.

Yes, Dixie had been forced to grow up and move on. She couldn't succeed otherwise. And she could not fail. That wasn't an option.

She could only guess that, to some extent, the same was happening with Joe. Oh, the core of him hadn't changed and never would. He would always be kind and generous, thoughtful and responsible. Sexy. But the world was a blank slate for him now. He would become more sophisticated, more worldly—like Jake and Donovan.

Not that she didn't adore Joe's brothers. She did. But they'd lived their lives entirely differently from Joe.

And they'd reached a time when they were ready to come home.

Someday maybe Joe would, too. But Jake had stayed away for almost twenty years first, and Donovan sixteen. A very long time. They'd both left town at eighteen, and their experiences had shaped who they were, whereas Joe would be going out fully formed and mature. She wondered if that would make a difference.

"I can hear how hard you're thinking," Joe said, the words rumbling in his chest in a way that almost brought tears to her eyes. It seemed so normal. Something they'd done thousands of times after waking up together.

He played with her hair, stretching out the curls then letting them bounce back. She loved how it felt, always had.

"Are you okay?" he asked.

She couldn't sing his praises too much. It would make it doubly hard to say goodbye in the morning. But she couldn't remember sex with him being so…elemental. Wonderfully so. Part of it came from a year of celibacy, part of it from knowing each other well, but also, they fit.

"I'm beyond okay," she finally answered.

"Me, too," he said.

"I could tell." She smiled. She hadn't been so relaxed in forever. "Thanks for thinking to blow out the candles." She rose up on an elbow so that she could see her bedside clock.

"What? We slept two hours!" She scrambled to sit up, panicked. Two hours of their night were gone. *Gone.* Never to be recaptured.

"Nice scenery," he said, laying his hands along her thighs and slowly massaging them. "Thank you."

Wasn't he listening? Wasn't he paying attention? They'd lost two hours by sleeping. Two whole hours.

His hands stopped moving. "What's wrong?"

She'd made a mistake by inviting him. They should've had a ceremony, like the one she'd envisioned, one involving kind words, good wishes for the future and a sincere thank-you and goodbye, perhaps shaking hands.

Not this. Not seeing each other without the trappings, but naked and vulnerable.

"You're having second thoughts," he said as she tugged the sheets up, covering herself.

She couldn't let him think that. It would only make things worse. "I'm cold. And kind of hungry. Are you?" She'd hardly been able to eat all day, between trying to figure out what to do about Joe and hosting the farewell party for Bitty.

"I could eat." He tucked her hair behind her ear. "You can be honest with me, you know. No matter what."

No, she couldn't. She'd already accepted the fact she loved him, would always love him. No good would come from her telling him that. She'd returned his ring—for good reasons—but even so, she refused to add guilt into his excitement over going out in the world and making his mark. It would be so much harder for him to go, knowing she still loved him. And he needed to go.

"I'm fine. Really, Joe. I think I was disoriented, waking up and having you here."

He gave her a good, long look, then took his cue from her. "Got some peanut butter?"

"I can do better than peanut butter sandwiches." She climbed out of bed, grabbed her robe from a hook inside her closet door. "Your family filled my refrigerator."

"That was a week ago." He pulled on his jeans and followed her to the kitchen.

"You don't understand. They *filled* my refrigerator,

freezer and all. I've got enough to live on for a month. Want some pot roast?"

"Mom's pot roast?"

She could almost hear him salivating. "None other. It won't take long to heat it up."

"The place looks good," he said, wandering around the living room. He picked up small items, some he would recognize, some new. She hadn't put up any photos yet, still debating about which ones. "Shana told me you had her refinishing furniture for you."

"Busy work." She slid the food container in the microwave and entered three minutes. "I gave her some money, and then was pleasantly surprised that she wanted to work it off."

"She's got pride, like everyone else." He leaned his elbows on the breakfast bar, watching her. "And dreams for herself and her daughter."

"I see that now, but *then* I thought she'd be the old Shana, the one who was selfish and self-centered."

"Maybe having a baby cured her."

"Good point."

"You still don't trust her."

She leaned across from him. "Not completely. I wish I could, but a part of me thinks she'll take off again. Depends on how Mom and Dad deal with it, probably."

"You can't stop her, if that's what she wants to do."

"I can try." She smiled, taking the sting out of the words. "She's my family. I want to know my niece. And, selfishly, I want to know they're both doing all right."

"She'll have to find work that pays enough to allow her to live independently. Hard to do without marketable skills, plus there's the issue of child care."

"That would be the case wherever she goes, though. At least here, she would have me. She needs me."

Joe didn't respond before the timer beeped. She pulled out the container, started to serve it up onto plates.

Joe stopped her. "Let's just eat out of the dish."

"Spoken like a true bachelor." Dixie clamped her mouth shut. What a stupid thing to say. Idiotic.

"Guilty. Come on. Just grab a couple of forks, and let's sit at the table."

They ate in silence for a minute, then he said, "I'm going to butt in here, Dix. You want Shana to need you. That's your M.O. You like being needed. I know it's hard, but you have to leave her alone. Let her make her own decisions. Even though you could make her life easier, resist, at least beyond survival basics, anyway. She'll thank you for it later. I get the feeling she's lived a pretty carefree life all these years. It's time."

It's time. The phrase echoed, having become common in Dixie's life. Nana Mae had said it. So had Joe. So had she, for that matter.

"I don't mean to tell you what to—" he began.

"No. No, it's fine. I was just thinking about what you said. I know you're right. It's just…"

"Hard for you."

She nodded, stabbed a carrot, but didn't eat it.

He curved a hand over hers and squeezed.

"I'm trying to change," she said.

"Not too much, I hope."

She almost said, "You, either," then stopped herself. She wanted him to be happy and fulfilled. If that required change, then okay.

That was the danger in knowing each other so well—change could be threatening.

"So, what was the reaction to your haircut?" she asked, needing to take the conversation down a different path.

"Shock. Laughter. Jabs. But mostly compliments. And everyone wanted to know who cut it."

"Did you tell them?"

"I changed the subject."

"So…everyone will guess it's me."

"Does it matter?"

She considered it. "I guess not. In fact, probably not at all. It will go a long way toward everyone thinking we've managed to end up with a friendship. They'll all feel less uncomfortable."

He picked up the food container and set it in the sink to soak. Dixie slid their chairs back in place. Suddenly Joe was there, behind her, wrapping his arms around her. She made herself relax, leaning against him, resting her arms on his.

"Could I interest you in a shower?" he asked, close to her ear.

"You could." She turned around and snuggled into him, enjoying the feel of his skin beneath her cheek, and the sturdiness of his athletic body. "We should probably figure out what time you should leave," she said. "Set the alarm clock. Just in case."

He rubbed his chin against her hair. "Five? Not too many cars on the road at that time."

"Okay." It was hours from now, but it wasn't enough.

"I still can't believe I'm here, Dix. It was a good idea to do this. It's helped."

Until tomorrow morning, she thought. They wouldn't really know until then whether this was a good or bad move.

But she would stick to her new plan to send him off with a kiss, a smile and a firm goodbye, because that was the point tonight. To say goodbye. To free each other.

Because it was time.

Dixie put on her slippers at five the next morning, completely aware of Joe waiting for her by the bedroom door. They'd slept now and then, brief snatches so that they could keep going, but she couldn't remember making love so many times in so many different ways before, not in one night. Sometimes tenderness had prevailed, sometimes it was intense and wild. Pleasing and satisfying—those were the unspoken rules, and they were followed.

He looked as serious now as she felt. He held out a hand to her. She took it, and they left the bedroom together. In silence they made their way downstairs and to the back door.

They faced each other, held hands. "Thank you," he said.

She nodded.

"Dix—" He stopped, seeming to struggle. "I feel… forgiven. I didn't know I needed to feel that."

Heat flared in her, the flames traveling head to toe, limb to limb, making her weak. She leaned into him. She thought she'd been prepared for this moment. Then he went and piled on feelings she hadn't known she'd had.

"I wasn't going to cry. I promised myself I wasn't going to cry." Her shoulders heaved, her voice shook. She could barely speak. "I didn't know I needed to forgive you until you said that. I didn't know I was carrying that around."

She felt him shaking, too.

"Live well, Joey," she said finally, pushing away from him. "Go forth and conquer. And have fun, too. You've worked so hard for so long."

He cupped her face, wiped her tears away and kissed her, softly, gently, until she wasn't sure she could bear it any longer. Then without a word, he left.

He was supposed to say goodbye. That was the point. So was she.

Neither of them had.

Chapter Twelve

"That's it. Get out. We're done." Dixie turned her back on the man she'd hired as her contractor. He'd finally come to her shop after she'd left him messages for three days.

"You can't just up and fire me, little lady," Bruno Manning said, puffing up his chest. "We got a contract."

"Which you've already broken. You were supposed to have secured the permits and started demolition on Monday. It's now Wednesday. *Night.* I've been working in the mobile RV when I didn't have to. I cleaned out the shop when I could've been working inside here, in comfort."

She crossed her arms and glared at him. "I made sure

I had an escape clause, because I'd heard you didn't always stick to the schedule. Page two, paragraph four. Read it."

Dixie grabbed a broom. She couldn't even look at him, she was so angry. She shouldn't be having to boss around a man old enough to be her father.

"I told you," Bruno said, towering over her, his size alone intimidating. "There were some problems. I couldn't get no one to issue the permits. We can't start till we do."

"You haven't even applied for the permits. I checked. So now you're lying to me, too." She'd been so determined to be independent, to prove her competence without help from any McCoy or even Kincaid. Now, right out of the gate, she was failing.

"You have nothing to say to that?" she asked Bruno. "I should've listened to those people—and there were many of them—who advised me against using you. So, now I'm going to listen to myself and get out while I can, because I can picture us having this same argument into spring. I've got a business plan, Bruno. You knew that. Most things depend on something else getting done on schedule."

He scoffed. "Hardly any renovation gets done 'xactly on schedule."

She knew that was true, but she didn't want to deal with him and his condescending tone a second longer.

"Maybe not. But they should *start* on time. Go away." She just wanted him gone.

"You can't tell me—" He stopped, tugged his ball cap down so far she couldn't see his eyes. "You ain't heard the last of this, little lady." He yanked open the door and stormed out.

"And don't call me little lady!" she shouted, raising a fist.

Someone started clapping. She whirled around. Kincaid stood there, a rare grin on his face.

Dixie felt her face heating. She started attacking non-existent dirt with her broom. "I didn't hear you come in. I suppose that's why Bruno left. I had backup, even though I didn't know it."

"I'd say he left because of you, tiger." Kincaid gently tugged the broom from her and set it aside. "Sit down, Dixie. Relax for a minute. Can I get you something to drink? I've got bottled water in my car."

"I'm too upset." She was glad he'd stopped by, after all. He was…soothing, she decided.

He sat in the chair next to hers.

She managed a smile. "I was sort of tigerlike, wasn't I?"

He rested his elbows on the chair arms, completely at ease. "Saber-toothed, I'd say."

"But that would make me extinct."

He laughed. She thought it was the first time she'd heard it.

"Well, you're rare, anyway," he said. "So. I didn't hear the whole confrontation, just the parting shots. What are you going to do?"

"I'm pretty sure I can break the contract, but I need to check with Laura."

"I can look at it, if you want. Or not," he added quickly, apparently seeing hesitation in her eyes.

"Laura drew it up, but thanks." She sighed. "I thought Bruno would come through for me. I'd heard the rumors about him, but I've known him all my life. He's done business with my parents forever. I figured he'd want to do right by me. And he does do very good work."

"He does. He doesn't skimp or cut corners. In that sense, he's a very good choice for anyone."

"Maybe anyone with patience." Which was in short supply these days for her.

"Here's a proposition for you," Kincaid said. "If you can get out of the contract, I'll take on the job at whatever he bid it for. And I'll guarantee it will be done on the date you specified."

"A smart man—one who'd made a certain bet with me—would delay it by at least one day."

His eyes twinkled. "I figure you might be appreciative enough of me stepping in during your time of need that you might give me free haircuts for a year, anyway."

"Kincaid, I would happily and gratefully give you free haircuts for life."

Something in him changed, his gaze turned… speculative, more intense, his laser-blue eyes direct.

"How about this?" he asked. "If I finish ahead of schedule, I still get free haircuts for a year. If I'm late, I'll throw in the new sign."

"That should make it fun." She didn't know how comfortable she was going to be, having him underfoot all the time. She could end up with problems bigger than the ones with Bruno. "I'll check with Laura and give you a call."

He didn't answer, but looked past her, then hopped out of the chair and went to the front door, opening it for Aggie, who pushed Emma's stroller inside.

"Thank you," Aggie said as she passed by Kincaid. "The snuggle-bunny here wanted to see her auntie."

Dixie laughed. "Did she say that? Are you talking now, sweet pea?" she asked her tiny niece after drawing back her quilt and getting a huge smile that melted Dixie's heart. She scooped Emma out of the stroller and touched noses with her.

"I need to get going," Kincaid said. "We'll talk later?"

"As soon as I have answers." She walked up to him. "Thank you."

He nodded. "Nice to see you, Aggie. Goodbye, Emma," he said formally, as if unsure how to talk to a baby. "Her eyes are as green as yours," he said to Dixie. "Beautiful."

With a final look, he left. Aggie was uncharacteristically silent.

After a minute, she came up behind Dixie. "I didn't mean to interrupt," she said.

"You didn't. We were talking business, but we were done." She bounced Emma, not wanting to turn around and face Aggie. Dixie had nothing to hide from Joe's mother—nothing was going on with Kincaid—and yet she felt guilty.

"Is that where your heart is leaning now?" Aggie asked.

Dixie shook her head. *My heart is taken.* "He's my landlord."

"You need to be careful there, Dixie. For his sake," she added, as Dixie turned around, ready to remind Aggie that she was a free agent.

"I haven't led him on," Dixie said instead.

"Maybe not consciously."

Great. So now she had to be aware of everything she did *un*consciously?

Aggie smiled and patted her cheek, then Emma's, in exactly the same way.

"I'm supposed to be moving on," Dixie said.

"Did I say otherwise? You know what it feels like to get hurt. You don't want Kincaid to go through that, do you?"

"Of course not."

Aggie nodded, as if that said everything. "Joe's staying up north longer than he expected. He decided to do the approaching instead of waiting to be approached. He's got appointments into next week."

"That's great." *Moving on.* Emma put both hands against Dixie's mouth and giggled. The desire to have her own baby hit Dixie like a lightning bolt. Maybe she'd been wrong when she'd told Shana her clock wasn't ticking. Maybe she'd just kept hitting the snooze button without realizing it, without hearing the alarm ring.

"Would you prefer I not talk about Joe?" Aggie asked, rubbing Emma's back.

Good question. She hated not knowing what he was

doing, hearing it secondhand, but… "I still care about him, Aggie. I want to know how he's doing."

"Even if he's dating someone?"

"Is he?" The words tumbled out before she could stop them.

Aggie clamped a hand on Dixie's shoulder. "I'm sorry. I'm so sorry. I was trying to gauge how much you wanted to know so that I don't tell you too much. That was dumb of me. I didn't mean to panic you."

Panic? Yes, that was exactly what she'd felt.

He hadn't said goodbye. That had been the purpose of the night they'd shared, and neither of them had said the word. She didn't know what to make of it. In her case, her throat had closed. She couldn't say it—or anything else.

"What do you hear from your folks?" Aggie asked.

Dixie latched on to the change of subject. "They're like a couple of teenagers. Mom loves the shows and the hustle and bustle of Las Vegas. Dad keeps winning at the slot machines, and I guess he's in tool heaven at the hardware convention. That ends tomorrow, and they're supposed to head to San Diego, which was their original destination, but who knows? They may get lost somewhere else."

"And they still don't know about Shana?"

"Um. It hasn't come up?"

"Speaking as a mother, I think you're making a mistake, Dixie. What if Shana takes off without seeing them? Without them meeting their granddaughter?"

"Aggie, your kids adore you. You've never been estranged from any of them, except for maybe some normal teenage rebellions, you know? Even Jake and Donovan checked in when they were gone. But anyway, it's up to Shana, not me. When I hear that Mom and Dad are headed home, I'll talk to her. I think the longer she's here, the better the chance she'll stay."

"You know your folks better than I do," Aggie said. "And your sister. Speaking of which, here she is now. I called and told her I would bring Emma to see you."

Shana looked good. Exceptionally good, Dixie decided as her sister scooped up Emma, laughing. The job had put her shoulders back and brought her head up.

Thank you, Joe. He'd seen that Shana needed her pride restored and done something about it.

It turned into a girls' night in. Aggie picked up Nana Mae and brought her back. They ate lasagna and garlic bread, and Shana told stories about customers at the tree farm, the other women trying to guess who she was talking about.

"Which woman," Shana asked, "waved off help sawing down her tree, then not only cut down an eight-footer herself but hauled it to her truck, loaded it and tied it down?"

All three women guessed, each getting a no for an answer.

"June Morrison," Shana said finally.

"June, the librarian?" Dixie asked. "That scrawny thing?"

Shana giggled, which warmed Dixie's heart in such hopeful ways. The dark circles were gone from Shana's eyes. She no longer looked gaunt, although still a little haunted at times.

When she stopped laughing, she asked, "Which man took three hours to choose a tree—and then only because I made the decision for him?"

"The mayor," Nana Mae guessed correctly. "That man is incapable of making a decision."

And so the evening went. At some point, Dixie sat back and surveyed the room. Women—and one baby—from four different generations, enjoying a good meal and some laughs. She'd forgotten her problems for a while. Hadn't thought about Bruno or the delay he'd caused or the confrontation with him—from which she'd emerged even more strong, confident and competent.

She'd forgotten about Kincaid, too, and how complicated he was making her life, even as he also simplified it. She'd even forgotten to call Laura and ask about voiding the contract.

What she hadn't forgotten, not for a second, was how much she missed Joe, missed him in ways she hadn't in the past year, because she'd spent so much of that time just being hurt and angry.

What she felt now was a different kind of ache that stayed with her, low and throbbing, even through everyday events like this evening. She watched Nana Mae cuddle Emma, who somehow knew she shouldn't squirm too much, who stared into the older woman's tender gaze and smiled. Dixie watched Aggie enjoying them, too. She'd been a doting daughter-in-law to Maebelle McCoy for a very long time. It was the relationship Dixie had always anticipated she would have with Aggie.

Shana caught Dixie's eye and smiled, as if to say, "This is good."

Dixie smiled back.

Later, when she climbed into bed, she ran a hand over the empty space next to her, remembering the night she'd shared with Joe. After a minute, she picked up her phone, started to dial his cell number to tell him about her evening with his mother and grandmother….

"Don't," she told herself, setting it down. "Let him be."

But it was so hard. He'd rarely been more than a ten-minute drive away, and even when she didn't see him, she heard about him, knew what he was up to. Now she didn't have a clue. He could be sitting in his hotel room, thinking about her. Or out with a woman who'd been forward enough to invite a handsome out-of-towner to dinner—or he could've done the asking.

Dixie stared at the ceiling for a long time, then she rolled over, pulled his pillow into her arms and held tight, knowing it was just wishful thinking that she could still smell him on the fabric.

Chapter Thirteen

"Pizza's here!" Dixie shouted. "Come and get it while it's hot."

The six men who'd been uncrating and moving salon equipment from a semi in her parking lot didn't knock her down, but only because she hopped out of the way in time. They were after the six large pizzas, three family-size salads and a whole lot of beer and soda she'd provided—the price of doing business, she thought, satisfied.

That and the muscle power of Kincaid, some volunteer McCoy men and a paid crew of two. In nine days, minus Sunday off, Kincaid and his team had demolished the shop, opened the wall to the additional space next door and were ready to replumb. Kincaid himself worked fourteen-hour days.

Dixie enjoyed watching the hardworking men dig into the food. She'd dragged sawhorses and sheets of plywood into the middle of the space to create tables, although they would have to stand while they ate. Four portable heaters took the edge off the cold December evening, but didn't really warm the place much. It was Friday night. The men were giving up personal time to be here, the truck having shown up four hours late.

Joe's brother Donovan leaned a shoulder against the bare stud next to her then took a big bite of pepperoni-and-sausage pizza, looked at her. "You're grinning like the village idiot."

"Every town needs one. Guess it's my turn."

He laughed. "Yeah, I suppose we all take turns, don't we?"

"What do you hear from Joe?" she asked lightly.

He looked at his watch. "My guess is he's pulling into his driveway, give or take ten minutes."

He's home. It'd been the longest twelve days of her life. "I imagine he's exhausted."

"I think he's on a success high," Donovan said. "He called as he was leaving the airport, all wound up."

She looked at her fingernails. "Does he have to leave again right away?"

"Looks like it. That's a sign of success, though, right? He'll be home again for Christmas. Fortunately, most city governments don't conduct much business then."

"Aren't you eating, Dixie?" Kincaid asked, joining them, leaning against the stud on the other side of her.

Her stomach was doing cartwheels. She wasn't sure she could keep anything down. Joe was home. *He hadn't said goodbye....*

Was that just a technicality?

"I'll eat in a minute," she said to Kincaid.

Shana stepped into the fray, still dressed for work in her heavy jacket, knit hat and mittens. Her cheeks were red, her eyes bright. She'd come so far in just a few weeks. "I was on my way to pick up Emma, then I smelled pizza."

"Have some. There's plenty," Dixie said. "I'll join you, now that the initial feeding frenzy is over."

"Kincaid is looking cozy," Shana said quietly, sending him an unfriendly glance.

"Stop it, Shana. He hasn't said or done anything improper."

"He wants to." She tugged off her mittens and stuffed them in her pockets.

Did he? Dixie went out of her way to keep things friendly but businesslike, not giving him any reason to hope for more. She wished she could. He was a great guy. She just didn't feel that way about him.

"So, I have news," Dixie said. "Guess who's coming for Christmas?"

The color drained from Shana's face. Her plate tipped, her pizza slipping. Dixie grabbed it, righted it.

"I'm sorry," Dixie said. "I was so excited, I didn't think. Not Mom and Dad. It's Gavin. Gavin's coming for Christmas. He'll be here Christmas Eve, actually. For the first time in years, our brother has not volunteered to be on call Christmas day."

"Does he know I'm here?" Shana asked, setting down her plate.

"That's why he's coming."

"What'd he say when you told him?"

"'It's about time.'"

Shana smiled and pressed her fingers to her mouth. "We were never close as kids, but I've missed him, you know?"

"I do know. I only see him a couple of times a year myself, and I live two hours away. But, you know, Shana, he did the same thing as you did. We just always knew where he was living."

"It must have been hard on you, being the one left behind, having to deal with Mom and Dad on your own all the time. Did you resent Gavin and me?"

"Sometimes. But what were my options? I didn't want to leave town."

"Never?" Shana asked. "You've never had a desire to see something beyond this place?"

"There are places I'd like to visit, but to move? Why? I love this place. It's home."

"Speaking of home, I need to pick up Emma. Thanks for dinner. And for calling Gavin." She gave Dixie a hug, then took off.

The men tossed their paper plates in the trash and headed back to the parking lot to bring the equipment into the newly created space, currently the storeroom.

She'd considered building separate rooms for each stylist but rejected the idea. Most of her steady clientele would be townspeople. They liked seeing who was passing by the shop, and liked being seen. It was a gathering place. People frequently stopped in and visited clients while Dixie was doing their hair.

She was still working on lining up renters for the other stations, as well as a massage therapist, manicurist and an esthetician. She wanted to create a fun but soothing atmosphere. It meant careful hiring, and she'd had little time, being busy in her temporary salon morning to night, then fulfilling her responsibilities at the hardware store. So much to do.

She was exhausted all the time, yet energized, too.

Because the men had told her to just get out of the way, she walked over to the front window and looked into the darkness. Streetlights illuminated the quaint wooden sidewalks and storefronts. Not much happened downtown at night. The Lode was open for dinner, and they were only a block up the road, so cars lined the street, but the ice cream shop next door shut down early in the winter months. There was little foot traffic.

Are you home yet, Joe? Will you call? Come see me? Did you miss me?

The men finished up and left, except for Kincaid.

"Can I take a few minutes of your time?" he asked.

"Sure."

He smiled. "Maybe upstairs, where there's better heat?" He tapped a rolled-up blueprint against his thigh.

"Oh. Of course. Come on up." He hadn't been upstairs since she'd moved in. It would be polite to offer him a hot drink. She didn't see how she could avoid it.

"Coffee would be good," he said when she asked, and because that took a little time, he sat at the counter, looking around the open space. She hadn't had time to hang photos yet, but Shana had taken care of everything else.

"The place looks nice, Dixie. You've made it a home."

"I'm very happy here." As soon as the coffee started to brew, she said, "So, what's up?"

"Do you know when Joe will be back?"

He's home. Just the thought of it got her heart racing. "Soon, I think. Why?"

"I'm still waiting for him to sign the papers. Normally it wouldn't be a problem, since listing a house in December rarely pays off. But I've got someone who's interested in it. At full asking price."

Dixie turned away, busying herself with getting out mugs. The thought of someone else living in her house had only been an idea before. The reality of it almost brought her down. "Have you called Joe?" she asked, trying not to let Kincaid see her hands shaking, but the mugs rattled as she set them on the countertop.

She saw him look at her hands, so she shoved them in her pockets, trying to look casual.

He studied her face for a few seconds. "I've called him several times, left a message each time."

"I don't know what to say." And she didn't. "I've done my part."

He sat back a little, watched her for a while, then, "Are you afraid to be alone with me? Do you think I'm after you?"

Aren't you? "It would be egotistical of me to say yes, wouldn't it?"

"Here's the thing, Dixie. I like you a lot. I haven't had a woman friend before, and I'm enjoying that. But that's all. When I'm interested in a woman, I like her to be looking at me. You're looking at Joe. Is that clear enough?"

Relief settled over her. "I like you, too."

"Okay, then. Business as usual."

"But better," she said and poured him a cup of coffee.

Joe huddled inside the recessed doorway of the shoe store across the street from Dixie's salon, his face stiff from the cold, his ears frozen, even with his collar pulled up. He'd gotten home, deposited his luggage in his bedroom, turned on the heat, thumbed through the accumulated mail, then left.

He wanted to see her. Needed to see her. But when he'd arrived, she'd had a shop full of people. At one point she'd stood at the front window, looking out. He'd willed her to see him in the darkness, but he'd been well hidden.

So he waited, watching a semi leave, then several cars, including Donovan's, but he could see through the plate-glass window, knew one person remained—Kincaid.

Fifteen minutes ago, her living room lights had come on. Kincaid's SUV was still parked out front. Which meant they'd gone upstairs. Together.

What did it mean? How long should he wait? Too many conclusions jumped in his head.

Under similar circumstances, Kincaid had left the scene—or so he'd said. Apparently, he was of stronger character.

Joe knew he should leave. It was like eavesdropping, when you never heard anything good. He didn't want to know if something was going on between them—and he *had* to know. He wanted to talk to her, to share how the trip went. He'd been busier than he'd anticipated. Had spent each night working in his hotel room, modifying each project to a particular city's needs. His ideas had been met with enthusiasm. He would make return trips after the holidays, after they'd had time to make decisions.

Every night he'd wanted to call and talk to Dixie about it. She'd been there five years ago when he'd first developed a plan for LandKind. He'd talked constantly about it to her.

And now, after a year of not sharing their day-to-day lives, he felt a need to do so. All during the drive from the airport, he'd been anticipating talking to her—

Hell. When had he started lying to himself? He wanted to take her to bed—and then talk. Maybe.

They hadn't said goodbye, either of them. Had she noticed? Was he making something of nothing?

He shrugged deeper into his jacket, debating again whether he should leave, not wanting to know if Kincaid spent an hour—or the night. A shadow passed in front of her living-room curtains, then another. A few seconds later, Joe saw them come toward the front of the shop. Kincaid came out the door and got into his car without looking back. Had they kissed upstairs? Were they officially dating?

Dixie locked the door, moved around the space, going from heater to heater. She went out of sight, probably to lock the back door, then the work lights went off one by one.

Joe waited for Kincaid to pull away, then jogged across the street and around the back. He rang the bell.

Seconds later, the door opened.

"You should ask who's here," he said, jealousy making him more curt than he had a right to be. He'd thought he wanted Dixie and Kincaid together. Craziest idea he'd ever had.

"I'd hoped it was you," she said breathlessly.

His doubts went up in flames. He reached for her, pulled her into his arms, kissing her as if he hadn't seen her in years. He couldn't get her close enough, his jacket like a wall between them.

"You're freezing," she said, leaning back and putting her hands on his cheeks, their warmth almost painful. "Come inside. Hurry."

They rushed up the stairs. He followed her into her bedroom, where she started stripping.

"What're you waiting for?" she asked. "I'm going to warm you up. Unless you'd rather have coffee. I just made a pot."

Her eyes were shimmering, a little laughter mixed

with a lot of desire. He caught up, finished undressing as she hopped under her covers, giving him barely a glimpse of the body that had flashed in his mind constantly, even during meetings.

He dove under the blankets with her, pulled her close, heard her gasp, felt her stiffen. "Sorry," he said, and he was, at least about being a human icicle against her, though not for anything else. He was where he wanted to be.

With their arms and legs wrapped around each other, their torsos touched, fire and ice, desire and need.

Ever so slowly, her heat transferred to him, through him. They didn't move for a long, long time, didn't say a word, just held tight.

"Your back's still cold," she said, sliding her hands up and down his body. "Roll over."

Because he would've followed her over a cliff at that point, he did. She curved herself behind him, tucking her legs against his, her free hand rubbing his chest, gliding down his body, then staying to linger. He'd already been aroused by the time he'd gotten in bed with her, a fact that couldn't have escaped her.

"Hmm. One area is warmer than the rest of you," she said, a smile in her voice.

"You must be wrong. Feels cold to me. Keep on heating me up." He closed his eyes, savoring her touch as she stroked and swirled, making him arch and reach and try his best to hold back.

"Just let go and enjoy it," she said, her lips against his neck.

But he wanted to be inside her. He knew her well. Knew she was as ready as he, knew she would climax almost immediately, the same as he would. So he took charge, rolled her onto her back, pressed his mouth to hers, and slowly pushed into her, feeling her clench around him, hearing her make low sounds in her throat.

"Don't go slow," she said, entreating him, digging her fingers into his rear, wrapping her legs around him. "Don't be gentle."

He didn't have to be told twice. He grabbed her hands, linked their fingers, held them above her head and gave her what she wanted and he needed, feeling pulled into an abyss of pleasure, dark and dangerous.

Dangerous. The word echoed in his head even as sensation inundated him, overtook him…devastated him.

He couldn't look at her, afraid she would see something he didn't want her to see. Dangerous? He never would have applied the word to her, not in any way— before. Now it was different. Now he knew she was still a danger to his heart, and his plans.

He rolled onto his back, taking her with him so that she blanketed him and he could keep her head tucked against him, not making eye contact. His heart pounded. His mouth went dry. He didn't want to talk. He hoped she would fall asleep.

He closed his eyes, let himself drift….

Dixie felt his body relax beneath her, but she didn't want to move. It was way too early to fall asleep, although she tried. After a while, he repositioned her more comfortably. "Do you want me to move?" she asked.

"You're fine. You feel good."

Now that she knew he was awake, she said, "We didn't say goodbye. Before. Last time. Either of us."

"I know."

So he *had* noticed. "It's been on my mind the whole time you've been gone, Joe. I've been trying to figure out what it means."

"Me, too."

"Is this something you expect—" she almost said *want* "—to continue?"

He was silent long enough that she regretted bringing up the subject—even though she knew she had to.

She moved off him, started to get out of bed, but he stopped her.

"I've been trying not to have expectations, Dix. I wasn't sure you would even let me in, much less sleep with me. So, did I expect it? No. Did I want it? I think the answer is obvious."

"So, now what, Joe? Where does this leave us?"

He threaded his fingers through her hair. "This probably seems crazy...."

"You want to continue," she said.

He nodded. "Until one of us *does* say goodbye."

"And when that moment comes, for whatever reason, the other person just accepts it? That's that?"

"Could you do that?" he asked.

He looked so earnest. Would he feel differently if he

knew she still loved him? Had never gotten over him? Had no interest in ever saying goodbye? "So, if one of us starts dating someone else, we say goodbye? Until then we meet for sex when you're home, but in public no one suspects?"

"Unless you have something else in mind."

"Do you seriously believe we can get away with that in a town that doesn't need security cameras? You don't think someone will see you arrive late at night or leave early in the morning?"

"It helps that you're in the business district, not a residential area. I'll be careful."

She thought she should feel used, but she didn't. She wanted what he wanted.

She also knew she was only delaying her pain, because he was bound to start dating someone before she did.

"Okay," she said, and waited for regret to follow. It didn't.

He pressed his lips to her temple. "So, tough girl, tell me about firing Bruno."

She told him about standing up to the man and how Kincaid had come to be her contractor. Joe told her about the people he'd met and the places he'd gone, wonder in his voice, pride, too, that his ideas were being so well received and respected.

She was happy for him. For years he'd researched and studied what he was promoting now. He'd tested his ideas in Chance City. Then when other towns in the area had heard about him, they'd hired him to teach them the same things. Community-wide compost programs were established in several cities, his brainchild, his dream. And now his name would become known far beyond their little town. She couldn't be more proud.

"Look at us, Dix," he said, well into the night. "Who would've thought it?"

"I always believed in you, Joe. Maybe more than you believed in yourself." But that was changing now. She could see it. See his confidence, acknowledge that he had become separate from her. It was happening to her, too, just as she'd predicted.

They had made the transition, had gone beyond being Joe-and-Dixie.

Now they were just another couple having an affair.

So where did that leave them? How could she say goodbye when what she really wanted was to say, "Be mine, forever."

Chapter Fourteen

By Christmas Eve, Dixie was running on fumes, fueled by vitamins and caffeine. Everybody wanted a cut-and-color for the holidays, and Dixie was trying too hard to be accommodating. She was aware of it, but couldn't seem to stop herself, knowing how fickle people could be. If they were forced to find another salon during the construction period, they might not return.

Dixie couldn't afford that.

So she scheduled appointments back to back to back. Her feet ached, her legs begged for mercy, even her hips were talking to her.

And Gavin was supposed to arrive soon, so she wouldn't have time for a hot bath.

Worst of all, Joe had gotten home that morning but they wouldn't be able to see each other because of Gavin, who planned to sleep on Dixie's couch for the one night he would be in town.

Joe would've given her a massage. Among other things.

She smiled at the thought. Two weeks had passed since they'd agreed to see each other secretly, which created a tension between them that they didn't discuss. He hadn't signed the paperwork to sell the house yet, either, something else they didn't talk about.

Kincaid had stopped asking, too.

Dixie dragged herself upstairs to her apartment, then the doorbell rang before she even got to her sofa. Her muscles protested every step she took down the staircase. She was grateful that Christmas came on a Saturday this year, which meant she wouldn't have to work for the next three days.

"Gavin," she said, smiling, when she opened the door. It didn't matter that he ignored his family most of the time—he was still hers.

"Dixie Rae." He grinned back, then picked her up and whirled her around. As blond as his sisters, his eyes the same Callahan-green, he was tied to Dixie and Shana by their shared upbringing. It was an unbreakable bond, even if it was ignored for months—or years—on end.

"You've lost weight," he said, setting her down, frowning.

"Just a little. But you would, too, if you'd been living

my life." He and Shana had always been naturally thin. "You look fabulous," she said.

"Do I? I shouldn't. I guess it's just seeing you."

She drew him inside and up the stairs. "Why shouldn't you look fabulous?"

"Usual doctor stuff. Long hours. Pressure from patients, staff, insurance companies, hospitals. Lawsuit."

"Lawsuit?" She turned around, walking backward into her living room.

"Malpractice. I'm not allowed to talk about the details."

"Even with me? Who would I tell?"

"I can't, Dix. The only reason I brought it up is because I've been pretty distracted, and I want you to know it's not personal if I zone out on you, okay?"

She hugged him until he hugged her back. "I'm sorry."

"Me, too. It's a mess." He let her go. "So, have you got some Christmas goodies to ply me with?"

"Every client I have brought cookies or candy or something fattening and wonderful. Let me get out of my work clothes, then I'll fix a little plate. Shana should be here in about an hour for dinner."

"I'm going to get my stuff out of my car. I like your place, by the way."

Dixie made a quick change into something more festive—a Christmas sweater and black pants—then hurried back into the kitchen just as the door opened.

"Look who I found wandering around outside." He had one arm around Shana and the other hand gripped Emma's carrier. "The rebel returns."

Tears brightened Shana's eyes. She clung to Gavin, who gave her such a tender look that Dixie almost cried, too. She was happy. Unadulteratedly happy. After all these years, they were together. Nothing could spoil the joy of the moment.

"You're early," Dixie said to Shana, opening a tin of Aggie's thumbprint cookies.

"Joe stopped by and saw how dead sales had been since noon. He sent us home, said he had nothing better to do." Shana grinned. "We weren't too sure about leaving him alone and in charge. We don't think he's ever run a credit card."

"Well, then, knowing Joe, he'll either shut down early or just give the trees away for pocket change." Dixie kept herself busy opening boxes and Baggies, choosing a few treats from each. But she was aware that Gavin had stopped setting presents around her tiny tree and was watching her. "What?" she asked.

"You're sleeping with him again."

Shana gasped. "You are?"

"Don't be ridiculous." Did she sound indignant enough? "Why would you say that, Gavin? Joe and I broke up for good. Didn't you hear?"

"I keep in touch with Donovan. Yeah, I heard. But I'm looking at your face and listening to your tone of voice, not just the words. You still love him."

"I will always love him, but hearts have room to love lots of people," she said honestly. "And since when do you keep in touch with Donovan?"

"Since forever. With Gideon Falcon, too. We started hanging out in kindergarten, you know?"

"Why didn't you come to their weddings?"

"I was on call."

"Uh-huh. You didn't want to mix and mingle."

"Maybe I didn't. But I've seen both of them. They get to the city occasionally. Nice change of subject, by the way. Smooth." He came up to the counter and grabbed a couple of cookies while she got the coffee brewing.

"There's nothing I can say about Joe, Gavin." Out of the corner of her eye she saw Shana looking speculative.

They settled in for dessert before dinner, falling into the sibling repertoire of teasing, insults and memories recalled, comfortable and fun. Emma was passed from person to person, but also set on the floor to play, now that she could roll over and could drag herself along a little. Almost six months old, she needed to be on the move.

"What are we doing about dinner?" Gavin asked after a while. "I need protein."

"I forgot! I was supposed to call Caroline McCoy when I was ready. She's catering Christmas Eve dinner for everyone as a fundraiser for her tuition. She's started paramedic school, did you hear?"

"Donovan mentioned it."

Dixie reached into her pocket then realized she'd left her phone in her jeans when she changed. "Be right back." She went into the bedroom and found it, discovering one missed message.

"Hi, Dixie! We're on our way home. Would you please go to the house and turn on the heat for us? See you soon! We've had the best trip, but we sure are glad to be coming home."

Hunched over as if struck in the chest, Dixie returned to the living room, holding out the phone. "Mom and Dad are on their way home."

"When?" Shana asked, her face turning white.

Dixie checked the time of the message. "She called an hour ago. She didn't say where they were, only that wanted me to turn on the heater, which means they can't have been far."

"They'll see my stuff. Emma's crib." Shana rose slowly. "I left dishes in the sink."

Dixie's phone rang. Joe. He knew Shana and Gavin would be there. "Hey."

"Your folks are home. Did you know?"

"I just discovered a message from them from an hour ago."

"They're trying to park the RV in the driveway, but your dad has needed a couple of tries."

"Can you stall them? I'm on my way."

"I can try." He hung up, not wasting any time.

"Joe's there," Dixie said, grabbing her coat. "He'll try to stall them. They haven't gone inside yet." She paused. "Maybe I should go alone."

"I'll go with you," Gavin said.

"Me, too." Shana stood straight, her shoulders back. "Maybe just me. It's my problem."

"One for all, and all for one," Gavin said. "Bundle up the baby. The parental unit awaits."

Joe was generally good at small talk, especially in his hometown. He pretty much knew everyone, could find something in common to discuss. With Beatrice and Malcolm Callahan, Joe only had Dixie in common, *had* being the operative word. Dixie had given him back his ring over a year ago. Joe hadn't talked to the Callahans since, hadn't seen them to talk to, even, except from a distance that no one seemed interested in closing. They hadn't been particularly close. Joe had always resented the way they'd treated Dixie, as if she were just any employee instead of their highly competent daughter, who was a good part of their success.

"Need some help getting lined up?" Joe asked, coming up alongside the RV, where Malcolm was leaning out the window, looking backward.

He stared at Joe as if he'd spoken in a foreign language. "That'd be good, thanks. It's too dark to see if I'm going to hit that old oak."

"Let me take a look. Hi, Bea," he called to her in the passenger seat. "Welcome home."

"Thank you. How's everything here?" she asked.

"Um, I'm not sure. I just got back from a ten-day trip myself."

Joe could tell Malcolm was impatient to be parked and done. Joe ambled to the rear of the unit. If Malcolm moved straight back about four feet, he'd be in good shape.

Joe walked to the driver's door again. "You need to pull back out and move it to the right about two feet."

"I do? Thought I had it okay."

"Not quite. I'll stand back there and let you know when to stop."

"All right, thanks, Joe."

It ended up taking a while, because twice Malcolm had to stop to say hello to neighbors walking by. Each time Joe held his breath, waiting for someone to mention Shana, but Malcolm brushed them off fairly quickly, reaching the end of his patience. Joe was surprised that Bea hadn't gotten out and gone inside.

He also wondered how Dixie and Shana were going to explain the situation. He knew that Dixie's original plan was for Shana to relocate before her parents came home, figuring they would have more advance notice than they'd gotten, obviously.

Joe spotted headlights, then recognized Dixie's car. He decided he'd better hang around in case they needed his truck to haul Shana's things.

"Oh, look! Dixie's here," Bea said, walking toward the car.

Three doors opened. Dixie got out, so did Gavin.

"And Gavin! What a lovely surprise!"

Bea picked up her pace. Then Shana emerged, carrying Emma. Bea stopped. Shana kept coming. Dixie and Gavin moved into position, flanking her.

"Hi, Mom," Shana said, her voice quavering a little, but otherwise strong. "Hi, Dad."

"Shana?"

"It's me." She took a step forward, away from her protective siblings. "And this is Emma, your granddaughter."

Malcolm had come up beside Bea, put his arm around her. "And where might your husband be, Miss Runaway?"

"Emma's father died. I know this is a shock to you, Mom. I didn't mean to spring it on you like this."

"Then why did you?" Malcolm bellowed. "Your mother doesn't need these kinds of shocks."

"Because you would've gone in the house and wondered who'd been living here. I'm sorry. I didn't get the breakfast dishes done before I left for work."

Malcolm turned on Dixie then. "You let them stay in my house?"

"She needed a place to go, Dad. There was nowhere else."

"Your mother talked to you several times on the phone. You never brought it up. Never asked for permission."

"That's true. Why don't we go inside where it's warm and we can talk about it."

"There's nothing to talk about," Malcolm said. "You, of all people, Dixie. To lie to us, after all we'd been through because of her? How could you? Come, Bea."

Joe watched it all from the sidelines, had guessed how it would all shake down. He wasn't surprised that Malcolm was turning his back on Shana—he was the most stubborn man Joe knew. But he was surprised to see Bea go with him. Even if she didn't want to talk face-to-face with Shana yet, there was Emma, the innocent child. Bea's granddaughter. Bea had been waiting a long time to be a grandmother.

"Mom!" Shana called. "Give me a chance to explain. Please."

Bea stumbled. Malcolm held her up, pulling her along and into the house.

Gavin put his arm around Shana. "They need some time, honey. It's a shock."

"I brought this on myself. I don't blame them," she said, wistful, then her chin came up some. "No, that's not true. It was their fault, too, that I left. Their fault I stayed away. I knew I shouldn't have moved in while they were gone. And now what about my stuff? And Emma's things? Her formula and bottles. It's Christmas Eve. I can't buy anything to replace it tonight or tomorrow."

"I'll get everything," Joe said. "You go back to Dixie's and stay warm. Get Emma inside."

"I'll help," Gavin said, following Joe.

Dixie sent Joe a look of gratitude. He didn't care what Shana and Gavin thought. He went over to Dixie and gave her a hug. "They'll forgive you," he said.

"Does it get tiring being my champion?" she asked, then tried to smile. "How many times have you defended me to them? You can't imagine how often I wished your parents were mine."

He didn't have a response to that. He joined Gavin, and they went up the walkway. He rang the bell. Gavin turned the knob, but it was locked.

"Dad?" he shouted. "Let me in."

After a minute, Malcolm opened the door a couple of inches.

"She's gone," Gavin said. "Joe and I need to get her things. The baby's things."

Malcolm opened the door and walked away. Joe felt sorry for all of them. They never talked to each other, never confided, never openly got mad, then made up. Nobody's family was perfect, including his own, but everyone in his family hugged and teased and supported—and argued and made up. He'd never gotten used to Bea and Malcolm's coldness.

"We don't need to take the crib," Joe told Gavin. "Dixie's got one."

They stacked things into baby blankets, tied them up as bundles, then emptied the closets of Shana's clothes, carried them to the truck and returned. Bea had gathered up Emma's bottles, formula and baby food from the kitchen and put them in a grocery sack.

"I couldn't see her face," Bea whispered to Joe. "The baby's."

"She looks like a Callahan. She's beautiful."

Bea nodded, then stepped aside.

"Shana's been through some kind of hell," Joe added as he passed by her. "My guess? She could use her mother."

Joe caught up with Gavin, who stood next to his father on the porch, neither of them speaking.

"Merry Christmas," Joe said, then headed to his truck.

"Yeah, Merry Christmas, Dad," Gavin said. "I'll be

here until tomorrow evening. You've got my number. And, by the way, I'm not taking Shana's side here. I just want us to be a family, a normal family. I know it's a tall order."

He got into Joe's truck, rested an elbow at the base of the window. "Thanks."

"Glad I could help. I figure Shana and the baby will be staying with Dixie." Which also meant he and Dixie couldn't see each other. "You're welcome to bunk at my house. I don't have a spare bed anymore, but the couch is big enough for you."

"Thanks, again. I'll take you up on that. I'm tempted to just drive home to San Francisco, but that won't accomplish anything." He was quiet for a couple of minutes. "You know why I don't visit often?"

"You're always on call?"

A surprised, appreciative laugh burst from Gavin. "You know why I'm always on call? Because coming home reminds me of growing up. I don't know how Dixie stands it. Never mind. I take that back. She had you and yours."

"Dixie also puts everyone else first," Joe said, not caring if that stung Gavin or not. Joe was tired of everyone taking advantage of her—and especially tired of her letting them.

"I get it, loud and clear. I was selfish enough to let her. I'll bet she always made excuses for why I hadn't come to some event or another."

"Yep."

"For Shana, too?"

"She didn't have to, not after a few years. Everyone stopped talking about Shana, as if she'd died."

"Dixie and I would talk about her sometimes," Gavin said. "Especially when the annual Christmas card arrived with a different postmark. We speculated a lot. And now here she is with a baby, and no father in sight."

"She says he died, that there are other living grandparents. She just doesn't talk about the man."

"Any bets she'll run off again and we'll never know the answers?"

Joe considered it. "I don't know. She seems to be finding a place here. Maybe it's just financial. She can't afford to go anywhere else. But she's also not the angry, scared woman she was when she got here."

He pulled into the parking lot behind Dixie's building. "I'm just going to drop off everything and go, Gavin. Come when you're ready. I'll leave the front door unlocked." He squeezed Gavin's shoulder. "I'm glad you're here. Your sisters need you."

"I'm here for twenty-four hours."

"Better than nothing," Joe said.

They hauled everything upstairs. Dixie had already made space in her closet for Shana's clothes.

"Would you like to stay for dinner?" Dixie asked Joe when they were done. "Caroline's on her way. She's bringing raviolis."

"I've got stuff to do. Ten days on the road…"

"I forgot! I'm sorry. How'd it go?"

"Very well, thanks. See you later," he said to everyone.

"I'll go down with you. So I can lock the door," she said.

"I'm not seeing progress here," he said at the bottom of the staircase.

"Plumbing and electrical. Tedious, but not something you'd see right away." She slipped her hand in his. "Thank you."

He squeezed her hand. "Your parents will come around."

"Maybe." She leaned into him. "Do you remember our first time, Joe?"

"First time? You mean, sex?"

She nodded.

"How could I forget it?" he asked.

They'd reached the back door. She flattened her hands on his chest. "Most people wouldn't have believed we waited so long."

"New Year's Eve. We were twenty. Almost twenty-one, even. We'd been going steady for almost seven years. Yeah, people would've been shocked to know that. What's your point?" He knew his tone was brusque but he was annoyed that he couldn't come back tonight, sneak into the house, make love to her.

"Remember how, once we'd done it, we couldn't get enough, and we had no place to go that was private and safe?" she asked, running her fingertips around his ears, along his jaw, over his lips.

Really? She was teasing him when there was nothing they could do about it? "We were both still living at home, Dix. It complicated things."

"Which was the reason we bought the house together. We needed our own place—"

"So that we could have sex as much as we wanted to. Needed to."

"Yes. I am reminded of that feeling now, because we're going to be denied until Shana finds someplace else to live. And now that we've…feasted again, I don't like having to fast."

"We'll figure out something. I could rent a hotel room. You could meet me."

"If I could manage a second of free time, that would be great. When do you leave again?"

"Not until the first Monday in January." He couldn't wait a second longer to kiss her. He'd been gone for ten days. He would be home for ten days. But this time, he might be celibate. He didn't like it. "We could use the backseat of my truck."

The doorbell rang. They jumped apart, then Dixie laughed shakily. "Caroline," she whispered. "Dinner."

He took off his jacket and held it in front of him. Dixie pulled open the door, her shoulders still shaking.

"Here you go," Caroline said, shoving the insulated container at Dixie. "Hey, Uncle Joe."

The "uncle" part was a joke between them, since he was only five years older than she.

"Gavin's here," Dixie said to Joe's niece. "Want to come up and say hi?"

"Can't. I've got two more deliveries. Will you be bringing him by Mom's open house tomorrow?"

"I don't know if we're going. Maybe. Thanks a lot for dinner."

"Thanks for supporting me." She waved and hurried off.

"I guess I should get this upstairs while it's hot," Dixie said.

"Just stick it next to your body."

She smiled, then went serious. "If I don't see you tomorrow, I hope you have a merry Christmas."

"I'll see you. Somehow. Some way."

"Gavin asked if we were sleeping together," she said. "I hedged."

He gave her a tender kiss, the kind they shared after sex when they were sprawled and feeling luxurious in their satisfaction.

"Sleep well," he said. "Sleep in. You deserve it."

"I'll try."

"Come to Mom's for a while tomorrow afternoon."

"I'll try."

He ran a hand down her hair then took off, craving her.

Have a merry Christmas?

Not likely, not with the ghosts of Christmas past keeping him company.

Chapter Fifteen

Through her closed bedroom door, Dixie heard Emma crying. Six a.m.

So much for sleeping in.

On the other hand, Shana hadn't slipped out during the night and left town. That was progress, and a huge relief.

Dixie tucked her hands behind her head and stared at the ceiling. Even considering the confrontation with their parents, the brother and sisters had enjoyed their evening together. Sometimes their conversation was serious—like how they felt as if they'd been raised by nervous, fearful grandparents instead of parents.

"Because they brought up teenagers so late in life?"

Shana had wondered aloud. "Dad was sixty-five when I left home. Mom was sixty-one."

The revelation came as a blow to Dixie. She was already thirty, only eight years younger than her mom was when Gavin was born.

Dixie had gone to bed last night thinking about it, had come to the realization she was making a mistake by hanging on to Joe. If she waited him out, let him go do the things he'd wanted to do forever, and he by some chance decided to come home again, how old would she be by then?

"Mom and Dad were old at twenty-five," Gavin had said at some point the night before. "They would've kept us on short leashes even then. It's just who they are."

He was probably right, but still…Dixie wanted to have her children when she was young enough to remember her own childhood, to go places and do things with them, to play and hike—

Well, she shouldn't go overboard. She'd never liked to hike, after all.

A tap came on her bedroom door.

"Come on in." Dixie saw Emma first, smiling as Shana held her up to the open crack. "Merry Christmas, sweet girl."

"Merry Christmas, Auntie!" Shana zoomed her in like a plane, landing her on Dixie's lap. "We made cocoa. Would you like some?"

Dixie ignored the sting around her heart. Cocoa.

Joe. Cozy winter evenings by the fire. "I would love some, thanks."

She played with Emma until Shana came back and climbed under the covers with Dixie. They watched Emma practice her rolling skills, cheering her on. Tears welled in Dixie's eyes.

"Hey," Shana said, grabbing Dixie's hand. "What's wrong?"

"I want one of those," she said, looking at Emma. "I'm so busy, Shana. I have the challenge of building a new business, then the scariness of getting it up and running, making it successful, keeping it like that. I have friends and family who love me. But I'm so lonely. It's selfish, wanting more when I already have so much. So many people have much less."

"What are you gonna do about it?"

Dixie had expected sympathy, not Shana's matter-of-fact question.

"The way I see it," Shana went on, "you have two choices. Try to get Joe back. Or let Kincaid into your life. Both are possible, although you'd have to sacrifice something for either man."

"Is there a plan C?"

Shana laughed. "Sure. You could adopt one of *those*." She nodded toward Emma, who was practicing to become an opera star, testing high notes and giggling.

"What do you think I'd have to sacrifice?" Dixie asked.

"With Kincaid? I get the feeling he's been storing up

a lot for the right woman. He'd probably be romantic and attentive and worship at your feet."

Except Dixie knew that wasn't true. "There's a downside to that?" Dixie asked, playing along.

"Isn't there always? The downside is that he wouldn't get that in return from you, which would be unfair to him. Because your heart has always been and will always be in the hands of someone else."

Which is exactly what Kincaid himself identified, smart man that he is.

"And when it comes to Joe," Dixie said, "either he would have to sacrifice his chance to fulfill his dream— or I would."

"Bad timing, huh?" Shana asked, sympathy finally in her eyes. "But if it were me, I'd go for love. Talk about lonely, Dix? Try being a single mom—even with all the willing help, the same as you talked about."

Dixie rolled onto her side, facing her sister. "Would you tell me about him, Shana?"

She sipped her cocoa first, stalling. Just when Dixie was going to change the subject, Shana said, "His name was Richard. We were both nineteen when we met, living in New York City. He was just like me, Dixie. We weren't even two halves making a whole, but just one. One. We'd both left home instead of going to our graduation ceremonies. His father was abusive. Richard said he came *this* close to hitting back, but decided to leave instead."

"Smart move."

"He was brilliant, and such a gentle soul. We cared

about the same things. We just wanted to breathe our own air. Does that sound silly? I don't know how else to put it. We traveled all the time, taking jobs to make enough money to live on, and then moving to the next place. We never planned to have children. Weren't interested in the trappings of marriage. What we had was pure and perfect."

Which sounded so much like Shana, Dixie thought. She'd always been a free spirit, but had been tied down by their parents' fears, stifled from being able to breathe, as she put it.

"He got sick." Shana's voice dropped almost to a whisper. "We thought it was the flu. We were working on a farm in Spain. He didn't think he needed to see a doctor, then his neck started to hurt. I got him to a hospital, but we'd waited too long. He died in my arms. Bacterial meningitis."

She started to cry. Dixie wrapped her arms around her and held tight, crying with her, feeling her heartache. Even Emma had stopped playing.

"Two weeks later I found out I was pregnant. It gave me purpose. I was so happy, Dixie. The people we'd been working for were wonderful, at first. Then when I wasn't able to do the work of two people they let me go. I made my way back to the States, lived hand-to-mouth, really, in bus stations and shelters. Had Emma in an emergency room. A women-and-children's shelter took us in for a few months. It was through them that I got the car, which some kind soul had donated. Then I came home."

"Why did you leave like you did, Shana? What happened?"

"A lot happened. I'm trying to put it in the past."

Dixie realized that was all Shana was going to say. Dixie hugged her tighter. "Promise me you won't leave again."

"I can't promise that. But I won't leave without telling you, and I'll keep in touch. There's not much here for me, you know? I need a job. I need to support myself and Emma. This isn't exactly the job center of the universe. With Christmas done, I won't even have the part-time work at the tree farm."

"It'll work out. Just be patient."

They spent a leisurely morning together, Gavin showing up around nine o'clock. They opened presents, fixed a big breakfast, then went for a walk, ending up at Aggie McCoy's for her holiday open house.

"Why, Dr. Gavin, how nice to see you," she said, pulling him into a huge hug, the only kind she knew how to give. "Doc Saxon's still looking for someone to take over his practice here so he can retire, you know."

Gavin laughed. "So I've heard."

"He's not getting any younger. We're all starting to worry about our medical care."

"Doc Saxon is still the sharpest scalpel in the operating room, Aggie. But nice try. I like San Francisco."

Except for that malpractice suit, Dixie thought. Wouldn't that be something, if Gavin could be talked into moving back to Chance City?

Crazy idea, she thought, dismissing it. He'd hated it here almost as much as Shana.

McCoys surrounded them. Dixie was used to it, and Shana was trying to adjust, especially when Emma got passed around like an appetizer plate, sampled then given to the next person. Gavin retreated to the family room with the big-screen television to watch football and catch up with Donovan and Jake. The three Falcon brothers and their families showed up, too. David Falcon had been Joe's best friend forever, but since he'd married Valerie, adopted her daughter and had a baby boy of his own last year, David and Joe hadn't spent much time together.

Dixie knew Joe missed that relationship. It seemed like everyone they'd been friends with was married and had children now. It was probably a big part of the reason Joe had expanded his business, was willing to be gone so much. He'd started to feel like an outsider in his own town. Having his brothers move home helped, except that they both were now married with children, too. It made a difference.

There were babies, toddlers and children everywhere Dixie looked in Aggie's house. Everywhere. The Falcons alone had eight. Dixie had attended the Falcon wives' bachelorette parties and weddings, been a bridesmaid in two of them. She knew Gideon's wife the least and sought her out now.

"I'm so glad you all came, Denise," Dixie said. "I wasn't sure you would, given how many of you there are now."

"We are a small tribe, aren't we? We don't match the McCoys yet, but I can see it happening with the next generation. I heard about your spa. That sounds great."

Shana joined them, looking overwhelmed.

"Yeah, big risk time," Dixie said to Denise. "But you know all about that. I heard you sold your business in Sacramento."

"I did."

"Shana, this is Denise Falcon. She's married to Gideon."

"Oh, the celebrity," Shana said, shaking her hand. "Your reputation precedes you."

"All in the past now. Gideon and I built a ski resort up north. That's my life now. That and our baby boy." She pointed to her husband where he stood holding a one-year-old towhead.

"Do you miss your life in Sacramento?" Dixie asked. "Miss your business?"

"Not a bit. Keeping the agency staffed was a constant challenge."

"Denise owned At Your Service," Dixie told Shana. "It's a high-level temp agency for clerical and household help. In fact, Denise met Gideon through her agency."

"My good fortune, and thanks to his brothers, Noah and David, who also hired women from my agency then married them." Denise smiled. "People nicknamed my agency Wives for Hire. It certainly turned out to be true with the Falcon men."

Wives for Hire? Dixie grabbed Shana's arm. "You could do that! You could work through the agency."

"I could?"

Dixie saw Joe come inside the house. He made eye contact. "Maybe you and Shana could talk about it?" Dixie asked Denise.

"Sure. You understand I don't own the business anymore, right?"

But Dixie barely heard the response. She went directly toward Joe—

She stopped before she got too close. What was she doing? She couldn't just walk up to him, like she had a right.

The realization pierced her. She turned around, made her way through the crowd to the family room and squeezed in next to Gavin on the couch. He raised a brow at her.

"Joe just get here?" he asked.

Dixie didn't bother to deny it.

"If he breaks your heart a second time, Dix, I won't turn a blind eye again."

She tucked her arm under his and leaned against his shoulder. "I appreciate the thought, but I can handle it."

"Well, if you want to get out of Dodge, I've got a spare room. Come crash with me."

"It sounds tempting, believe me. But I've got a business to run and a business to build. Doesn't leave time for much else."

"You take Sundays and Mondays off from the first

one. And certainly Kincaid doesn't need you around every second while he works. We'll play tourist. Ride the cable cars, stroll along the Wharf, eat crab until we're sick. Doctor's orders."

"Thank you."

"You're my sister. I worry about you. And I love you."

"I love you, too." She cocked her head at him. "Are you sure you don't want to take over Doc Saxon's practice? You'd be on call twenty-four-seven, the way you like it. Mom and Dad would be only a few blocks away."

"Why do you hate me, all of a sudden?" He nudged her shoulder playfully, then focused on the door. "Who's that?"

"Caroline McCoy."

"Really? What happened to the glasses and braces?"

"Geez, Gavin. You're remembering her from ten years ago." Dixie watched him check her out completely. "Go ask her about paramedic school."

"I think I'll do that. You're okay now?"

"Yes, big brother. Thank you."

"And you'll come visit me in the city?"

"Yes, big brother."

He grinned. "You think you're annoying me with that big-brother stuff. Well, here's a news flash. I like it." He patted her knee then headed to where Caroline stood.

Joe inched by them, heading straight for Dixie. She felt trapped, which must have shown on her face.

"Sorry," he said, crouching in front of her. "But your mom is waiting in your parking lot. I spotted her car and stopped. Your father doesn't know she's there. He's taking a nap."

"Thank you." She squeezed his arm briefly. "Merry Christmas."

"Same to you. Call me later."

She hurried up to Gavin, who opted not to go with her, then she got Shana and the baby. They walked quickly, Emma crying the whole time. She'd been asleep in Aggie's arms, the transition to the cold outdoors waking her. As they came into the parking lot, Bea got out of the car.

Dixie didn't know what to think. She could only hope. But Shana didn't slow down. She pushed Emma, still fussing in her stroller, toward Dixie and headed right into her mother's arms and was enveloped.

"I'm sorry, Mom. I'm so sorry."

"Me, too, Shana. Me, too."

Dixie had never seen her mother cry before. It made her cry, too.

Shana clung to her and wept. "I didn't know until I became a mother myself how much I hurt you."

Dixie lifted Emma from the stroller and held her close, trying to soothe her, but she wouldn't stop crying, either.

Finally Shana stepped back and held her mother's hands. "Come meet your granddaughter."

Dixie didn't stay long. She left, giving them time to work things out together. She didn't have any illusions that everything would be perfect between them now—

and there was still their father to deal with—but it was for Shana to figure out.

She didn't want to go back to Aggie's house, even though Gavin was still there, so she sent him a text message saying she was going for a walk and would see him back at her apartment later. She pulled her knit cap over her head, tugged on her gloves and started walking.

At night the town was a wonderland of Christmas lights, but during the day it looked a little desolate, with barren oak trees and dirty snow along the sides of the road. The small storm that had come through a couple of days ago had brought just enough snow to dust everything, but was mostly gone now. She loved winter weather—if she didn't have to drive anywhere.

Dixie sighed, creating white-frosted air in front of her. All in all, her life was good. She should be happy. She'd known why she wasn't for the year that she and Joe were apart, but in some ways it was worse this time.

Their new arrangement wasn't working, at least not for her. Hearing Shana's tragic love story made Dixie realize she was wasting time on a relationship that wasn't going anywhere. She wanted to love like Shana had—publicly, with her whole heart, until death do us part.

A car slowed down on the street, keeping pace with her until she finally glanced over at it. Kincaid. He rolled down the passenger window. She leaned close and smiled.

"Need a lift?" he asked.

"I'm good, thanks. Merry Christmas."

"Same to you. I suppose you've been partying with the McCoys."

She nodded. "And my sister and brother. He's here for the day."

"Gavin? I haven't seen him since graduation."

Chance City was indeed a small world. "How are you spending your day?"

"At the moment, by taking a drive." His smile didn't reach his eyes. He looked lonelier than ever.

It was too bad they hadn't hit it off, she decided. She liked him a lot. "My parents got home last night."

"Yeah? How'd that go?"

Dixie shook her head. "You're the only person I know who doesn't hear all the gossip a minute after it happens."

"I'm not on anyone's speed dial, I guess. Is Shana okay?"

Dixie wondered why Shana was so suspicious of Kincaid. He'd been nothing but polite to her. "It wasn't a good scene last night, but she's with Mom now. I'm hopeful. And she might be able to line up some work through Denise Falcon's old business, At Your Service. If that means Shana will stay, I'd be thrilled."

"That's great news. Sure I can't give you a lift? Or take you for a drive? You look like you need a break."

"Do I? Sorry. I let down my guard with you, I guess."

"I'm glad. It's good. Take it easy, okay?"

She waved as he left, then she struck out again. She didn't know how long she walked, but she ended up in front of Joe's house. Her house. Theirs. Still no For Sale sign out front.

It hit her hard then—she hadn't been moving on, something they'd both decided they needed to do, but neither had he. He'd gone away, conducted business, but he hadn't made the break. He hadn't even put the house up for sale.

If he wasn't going to be the one to say goodbye, she needed to.

Dixie hunched her shoulders against a sudden cold breeze. The air filled with the promise of snow, a smell unlike any other. Within an hour, she guessed.

She heard a car approaching, turned and spotted Joe's truck heading up the street. Had he been looking for her? He hadn't stayed long at his mother's house. Why? Had he gone in search of her?

That had to stop. She knew it without question now.

He pulled into the driveway beside her. "Want to come in?"

Not yet. I don't want to say goodbye yet.

But she'd made her decision. *It's time.* She could hear Nana Mae saying the words.

Dixie nodded. A minute later they were inside the house. Just the two of them.

For one last time.

Chapter Sixteen

Joe recognized right away that Dixie was in an odd mood. At first he thought she was upset about something and was trying to keep it inside. Then he realized she was calm, too calm, something he hadn't seen in a long time. She'd been running on determination and drive for weeks.

Added to the fact she'd been out walking by herself—and standing in front of their house—put him on alert. He headed to the fireplace to stir it up, avoiding whatever was going to happen next, because it didn't seem like she wanted to hop in bed.

"Joe."

Now he knew for sure. Her tone of voice clued him in. She wasn't here to sleep with him.

"It's time," she said.

He didn't question what it was time for. She was saying goodbye. Something had happened since last night when they'd kissed at her back door and she'd seemed as anxious as he to find a private place. But not now.

Worst of all—she was right. They'd dragged out their goodbye long enough, maybe too long.

"Is it Kincaid?" he asked, needing to know.

"It's *me*."

He nodded, came toward her. Her arms hung loose at her sides. She didn't cross them to prevent him from getting close or shove her hands in her pockets so that she wouldn't touch.

"So, this is it," he said.

"We want different things. Well, we both are looking to achieve success, but in different ways. We need to be free to find them. What we've done these past few weeks is kept ourselves in limbo. It's too hard. There's no movement. We're both people who are in motion all the time, whether it's work or play. Yet we've both become static."

"You're right. But it doesn't make it any easier."

"No."

He searched her face, saw the pain in her eyes that matched his own. "So, what do we do here, Dix? Have the ceremony we talked about before? Shake hands? Say good luck and see you sometime?"

She looked around the room. "This is a good place to end it, don't you think? Here, in this house we created out of almost nothing?"

"How about in the bed we shared?" He didn't think she'd say yes, but he needed to give it a shot. Other dreams had come true, so why not this one?

She nodded. "Yes. Yes, that would be good."

Joe knew right then he would have to sign the paperwork to sell the house. Too many memories would linger.

With a wistful smile, she took his hand and headed toward the bedroom. Once they reached it, they pulled back the quilt, then faced each other. He felt as much passion for her as he ever had, and yet felt the need to temper it more, afraid his feelings would get in the way.

"Wait," she said, when he started to pull her sweater over her head. She was shaking, as if it was their first time. "When we're done, I'm not going to linger. I'm going to get up, get dressed and go. Please don't follow me to the door."

"All right." He undressed her more slowly than any gift he'd ever received, appreciated what was under the wrappings more, too. He found it wasn't difficult to take things leisurely, even when she undressed him in return, her hands gliding over his body.

Their familiarity with each other meant they not only knew how to arouse, but how to delay satisfaction. She did things with her fingers that had him reaching, then she backed away only to use her mouth instead, stopping just before he hit the point of no return.

He returned the favor, while also memorizing every moment. The weight of her breasts, the texture of her nipples in his mouth, the smooth skin of her abdomen and the slick heat beyond. They teased and tormented in the ways they knew best....

But it had to come to an end. They couldn't continue much longer, couldn't hold back forever.

He moved above her. She welcomed him with her body, but her eyes were saying, "Stop. Wait. Not yet."

He couldn't wait. *They* couldn't wait. She'd been brave enough to make this happen, he needed to see it through.

He pressed into her, savored her warmth, bent to kiss her, deeply, eternally. They found a rhythm together, hit the peak at the same time, held suspended beyond anything that had happened in the past, then he lowered himself to her and burrowed his face in her neck.

The hands of time must have kept moving, but Joe couldn't measure it. After a while—a short while—she got out of bed and put on her clothes, not looking at him. He didn't take his eyes off her.

Then she leaned over the bed and kissed him. "Goodbye."

His throat spasmed. "'Bye."

He heard the front door shut seconds later. "Have a good life, Dix."

In a little while he would go find someone to talk to, although he didn't know who yet. Soon.

But first he needed to grieve.

Dixie didn't know where to go. She was a helium balloon set free, susceptible to the elements, ready to burst at the slightest impact. She walked without direction, came to a spot overlooking her parking lot. Her mother's car was still there.

She stood staring at it, getting colder by the second. The snow she'd predicted started falling, blurring her view. Her phone rang, jarring her. Hesitantly she pulled it out of her pocket. It wasn't Joe.

"Hi, big brother."

"Why are you standing in the snow?"

"How do you—"

"I'm looking right at you, Dix."

She saw him then, waving at her from her parking lot. "Are you leaving for home?" she asked.

"I don't know. Am I?"

She frowned.

"Do you need me?" he asked into her silence.

"Yes." The word came out like sandpaper along her throat, aching with unshed tears. "Yes. Please."

"Don't move. I'll be right there."

She couldn't move anyway. Her feet felt stuck in concrete.

Not half a minute went by before Gavin was there, helping her into the car. He drove off, covering both her clenched hands with one of his.

"Hang on. I'm taking you where no one will drive by."

She nodded, staring at their hands, swallowing hard. She lifted her head when she felt the car leave the paved road. They bumped along on dirt and rocks, snow falling in big flakes now, pretty but not enough to hinder their drive.

He parked in a grove of evergreen trees, left his engine running and the heater pushing hot air.

"It's over," she said. "We're done."

"He—"

"No. I did it. I had to." She looked into her brother's sympathetic eyes. "But it hurts…so…much."

He drew her close, wrapped her up and let her cry, not trying to soothe her, not saying anything at all, just being there, her port in the storm of loss.

"We've been sleeping together," she said after a while. "It wasn't smart, but it was necessary."

"Then it *was* smart."

She leaned her head against his shoulder, pressed a crumpled tissue against her cheeks and smiled shakily. "Now, tell me what you really think, not what a brother should say to a sister who's hurting."

"I think you're one helluva woman, with a big, tender heart that's got a crack down the middle. If I could write you a prescription for it, I would. But I do know this— time will heal it."

"So the saying goes. Will scar tissue be a problem?"

"Not for you. You'll love again, because that's who you are. And someday you'll be able to see Joe and it won't hurt."

"Promise?"

"I promise."

They sat for a while longer, talking and watching

the snowflakes drift. "We should probably go before the snow becomes a problem for you driving home," she said.

He backed out. She looked around, trying to figure out where they were. "Is this where you brought girls to make out when you were in high school?"

"Yeah. Ah, the memories."

She laughed. It felt good. "Is there no one special in your life now?"

"Do you know how many women won't date a gynecologist?"

"Is that a rhetorical question?"

He smiled at her. "You're feeling better."

"Yes. Thank you." She rested her arm across his shoulders. "Is there anything I can do for *you?* You really can't talk about the lawsuit?"

"I really can't. If that changes, I'll let you know." He pulled into her parking lot, made her promise to visit him in the city and then drove away.

Her mother's car was gone.

Dixie climbed the stairs, worn out, wishing she could be alone. Maybe Shana would move back in with their parents.

Wishful thinking.

Dixie found Shana asleep on the couch, Emma curled up with her. Dixie smiled at the picture they made, then she shut the bathroom door and ran a hot bath, adding bubbles.

In some ways she already felt lighter. And starting

tomorrow she would be busy again. She would bury herself in work for now. The future would take care of itself.

"Did I wake you?" Joe asked, crouching at his grandmother's feet. He'd found her dozing in her rocking chair, looking peaceful. He'd come to her hoping to find peace for himself.

She smiled. "It wouldn't matter if you did," she told him. "I can sleep anytime. The big holidays tire me out, even as I love them, love seeing everyone."

He pulled up a footstool to sit next to her. "Where's Caroline?"

"I don't know if she's still at Aggie's or elsewhere now. I told her I didn't need anything."

"Have you liked having her here?"

"Oh, yes. She's quite different from Dixie, of course, but efficient and attentive." She cupped his chin. "What's wrong?"

"Dixie and I broke up for good."

"Ah. I see."

"I'm telling you because—" He stopped. "I don't know why."

"Of course you do."

He found he could smile. "Enlighten me, please."

"You and I have always had a special bond, haven't we? You were the last born, the one who usually gets the least attention. I made it my purpose to make sure you got lots."

He hadn't known that was her purpose, but he had always felt deeply loved. "You made me feel special."

"You *are* special. Joseph, you held this family together after your father died. You shouldered burdens even when it stopped being necessary. Your sisters all have husbands who love and take care of them. Aggie came out of mourning for your father and has gone on to live well. She's happy." Nana Mae patted his shoulder. "It's your turn, just as it's Dixie's turn. She's done the same as you—shouldered the burdens of her family, trying to fill the empty spaces left by her brother and sister, feeling responsible for everyone's happiness. You two are peas in a pod. Why do you think you've always sparred so much?"

"It hadn't occurred to me."

"You've broken up before, and she's always taken you back. Why do you think it's different this time?"

"We said goodbye."

"Ah. Are you wanting advice, Joe?"

"I want some peace."

She nodded. "Okay, then. Have faith."

He frowned. *That's it? Have faith?*

Nana Mae smiled. "Sounds too simple, doesn't it? I've lived fifty-nine years longer than you. Trust me on this one, Joseph. Have faith. What's meant to be, will be."

"I like simple," he said, already feeling a little more peaceful. "You're a very wise woman."

"I'm like everyone else. I gained wisdom by figuring out how to fix something I broke. You will, too."

He fixed her a pot of tea, shared Christmas cookies and a game of Yahtzee with her. And when he went home, he slept, long and well.

He had faith.

Chapter Seventeen

"Free haircuts for a year, that was the deal, I believe, Ms. Callahan," Kincaid said, polishing a chrome towel rack in the sparkling new salon, Respite. It was Saturday, the day before Valentine's Day, her target date to open for business.

"As I told you three months ago, Mr. Kincaid, you got 'em for life," Dixie said, admiring the room. It was everything she'd dreamed of—and then planned for. "You'll be here during the grand opening later?"

"Definitely. I haven't done a lot of commercial work. It'll be good to show off what I can do." He gathered up his toolbox for the last time. "So. Today the grand opening. Tomorrow, your first wedding party and Valentine's Day. Any plans for yourself?"

"A full night's sleep?" She grinned. "Mom and Dad are leaving town today—and I'm done filling in for them. They're finally going to trust Doug. *And* Mom convinced Dad to let Shana and Emma stay at the house, even though he's still not talking to her. So, I'll finally have some time alone."

"It hasn't been easy."

"Not for any of us, frankly. But Shana's getting more work through At Your Service all the time. She's saving for a deposit on an apartment. It'll work out. It'd be good if Emma could have one day-care provider instead of being farmed out to various volunteers, but that'll happen, too. If Shana was living in Sacramento, she'd have more work but less child care available, at least for free. She's holding up well, though."

"Good. I'll leave you to enjoy your space for the hour you have left before you officially open the doors."

"Okay. Thanks. Really, Kincaid, thanks for everything. I can't begin to tell you." She choked up.

"I only facilitated, Dixie. It was your vision." He headed to the door. "Oh, I almost forgot. I'm showing the house this afternoon. These people have been prequalified, so if they like it, chances are the sale will go through, unlike the other times. Now that Joe's going to be gone for at least six months, it'd be nice if it worked out this time."

Dixie felt gut-punched. Six months? What? "What do you mean, he's going to be gone?"

Kincaid's jaw twitched. "I'm sorry, Dixie. I assumed you knew."

She shook her head. And apparently she was the last to know, if even Kincaid was in on the news.

"I heard he got a job overseas somewhere. See you," Kincaid said, making a quick exit.

Overseas? Why hadn't she been told? And what kind of a job would take six months? The world's largest compost heap? Going for a Guinness-book record?

How could it have stayed a secret? Even though she and Joe had been communicating through Kincaid the past six weeks, didn't she deserve a call about a momentous event like this?

She'd seen Joe several times since they'd said goodbye, but they hadn't spoken. She'd buried herself in work, feeling stronger every day.

Until now. Until hearing he would be gone for six months. Overseas. She wouldn't even hear any gossip about him. Nobody would. Whatever he was doing, he would be there long enough to meet someone he could get serious about. Fall in love with.

She'd known the day would come. She hadn't known how little prepared she truly was for it. She'd only hidden her feelings behind work, exhausting herself.

Dixie prowled the rooms of Respite, looking for the calm that the advertisements promised. She scanned the open front room with four chairs and three sinks, was pleased with the manicure/pedicure station in the back and the elegant products display up front. She moved on to a separate area with dryers, the private rooms for massages and facials, a dressing room for brides and bridesmaids, with makeup stations. There was also a quiet room, and a spa tub that held two clients.

She'd found great people to work for her, even backups for when necessary, had made arrangements with two local bed-and-breakfasts to put together package deals.

Dixie felt prepared and raring to go—and vaguely dissatisfied, now that she was done. It was normal letdown, she knew that, but it surprised her, anyway.

It probably had more to do with the news about Joe.

The bell on her front door tinkled. "Dixie? Are you here?" someone called out.

"Hey, Sharlene. How's the bride-to-be?" Dixie asked, shaking off her gloom as she moved into the main salon.

"Nervous. Excited. And it's not going to rain!" The twenty-year-old redhead flashed a bright smile. "Is it all right if we bring in the gowns now and leave them here overnight? My aunt is going to steam them, and we thought it would be better to do it here and leave them hanging."

"That's a great idea. Plus, having them on display in the bride's room will show people the possibilities."

"Everything will be locked up tight, right?"

"I'll sleep in that room tonight, if it'll make you feel better, Sharlene."

"Okay!" She laughed then. "I'm kidding. Just nervous about everything. Aren't you? I mean, about the opening? Everything looks beautiful."

"Thanks. I'm not nervous, but I am anxious for everyone to see it all done. And hopeful that there will be enough business to keep it afloat."

"Well, you can bet that I'll be telling everyone to come here. I'd better run out and let my mom know we can bring in the dresses."

"Have her drive around back. I'll meet you there."

Dixie's day sped by. People came and went. Cookies and punch were devoured, compliments paid, appointments made. Dixie paid Shana and Caroline McCoy to take people on tours, to make subtle sales pitches, which resulted in the booking of two bridal parties and several husbands purchasing spa packages for their wives as Valentine's Day gifts.

She'd done what she'd set out to do. It looked like the venture would be an initial success and word of mouth would keep it going at full steam. A lot of women—and men—who usually went to Sacramento for cuts said they would switch if she could keep later hours. She polled the other stylists, who agreed to work two nights a week until eight o'clock. Problem solved.

The last guest left. Shana gathered what remained of her belongings and went to their parents' house for what would be at least a month.

Dixie was alone. She'd been running on adrenaline all day, and now it dissipated in a hurry, leaving her drained. Tears of exhaustion filled her eyes. She let them fall, acknowledging the value in doing so.

She checked each room, but Shana and Caroline had

kept everything in perfect order. There wasn't a punch cup or a paper napkin in sight.

Finally she moved into the bride's room, where five dresses—one white, four Valentine-red—hung from hooks placed high enough that the gowns' hems didn't touch the carpet. One wall was completely mirrored.

Dixie used the sink to wash her face and hands then lifted the wedding gown down and held it in front of her, her red boots two bright spots at the hem. The design wasn't one she would've chosen for herself, but it was perfect for the vivacious, petite Sharlene.

Dixie moved to put the dress away then spotted Joe framed by the open door. Her heart did a somersault— out of surprise but also because she hadn't been so close to him since Christmas.

"How long have you been standing there?" she asked, lifting the dress up to its hook, aiming for nonchalance.

"A few seconds. Sorry if I startled you." He came into the room. "I wasn't sneaking around."

"What do you want?"

He didn't answer right away. "I just wanted to see the end result. It's impressive, Dix. You did it."

In more ways than one, she thought. She'd finished the salon, she'd broken free of her parents' hold, and she'd almost gotten Joe out of her system.

Almost. She hadn't quite made it yet, although not seeing him for six months should finish it for her. But right now she wanted to run into his arms.

"Kincaid said he was showing the house again

today," she said, wishing Joe would move so that she could get past him and into the main salon, where anyone who walked by could see in, where she had to keep her distance. She clenched her hands instead.

"I haven't spoken with him."

She stayed silent, waiting for him to tell her about leaving for six months, glad Kincaid had, even unintentionally, prepared her for the blow. She could keep her cool, offer her congratulations and let him think it meant nothing to her.

She had her own business now, her own success to worry about, after all.

And bills to pay. Big bills. Everything was dependent on her keeping the appointment books filled.

His phone rang. He looked at the screen, said "Kincaid," then took the call. "Okay... Actually, I'm with her right now. I'll call you right back."

Joe looked down for a second. "Your lucky red boots were hard at work today," he said. "Kincaid just got an offer—for the asking price."

A lead weight dropped into Dixie's stomach. "Suddenly, it's real. No room for haggling. No reason to delay."

"I know what you mean." He hefted his phone. "So, should I tell him okay?"

What if they're terrible people? she wanted to ask. *What if they ruin the beautiful garden? What if? What if?*

She had to know. "I need to ask him something first," she said, then found Kincaid's number and dialed. "Who's making the offer?" she asked.

"The new youth pastor for the community church and his bride. They just got married. She was ecstatic about the garden. Apparently, it's her passion."

"Oh."

Kincaid made a sympathetic sound, then added, "You can't get a better offer."

"I know." She tipped the phone down. "Okay?" she asked Joe.

He nodded, but he looked as upset as she felt. It was stupid to feel so attached to a house, but it had barely been a shell when they'd bought it. They'd turned it into a home, a real home, transformed by loving hands.

But whatever tiny, niggling hope she'd had that he would change his mind about them getting back together was shot down by his agreeing to sell the house. That was the clincher.

"Let's do it," she said to Kincaid.

"They want a thirty-days-or-less escrow," Kincaid replied.

"Thirty days or less?" she asked Joe.

"Not less."

"Thirty days," she relayed.

"Would you like to meet them?" Kincaid asked.

"Not me. Do you want to meet the people?" she said to Joe.

"No. Yes. Yes, I would."

"Joe wants to."

"We'll wait for him here at the house," Kincaid said.

"Okay, thanks." She relayed the information to Joe,

then they walked side by side to the main room. Her shoulder bumped his arm as they passed through the doorway. She felt electrocuted by the touch.

Not again. Her pulse pounded in her ears. She knew he'd said something, but didn't hear him. "What?"

"I asked if you had a date tomorrow for Valentine's Day."

She was still annoyed that one simple brush of their bodies had sent her soaring with need for him, and even more upset that he hadn't told her he was leaving the country. "How would I have a date, I'd like to know? All I've done is work. Work, work, work," she said, gesturing to the room.

And you've been off having fun, she wanted to add but didn't.

He held up his hands. "Sorry. I was just curious, that's all."

"Did you have something else to say, Joe?"

He hesitated, which made her heart pound again, in a way that Edgar Allan Poe would write about. Thunderous. Ominous.

"I need to get to the house," he said. "'Bye."

Just like that he was gone. Without telling her he was leaving the country. Completely leaving her out of his loop, as if she didn't matter.

She felt like throwing things, but went upstairs instead and grabbed a carton of mint-chip ice cream from the freezer and a big spoon.

She was halfway through it when the phone rang.

What now? She wanted to be left in peace, to wallow, even though she should be celebrating.

But she answered it, because it was impossible for her to resist.

"Dix? You need to come meet these people."

"No."

"Yeah, really. You do. Come now." He hung up, leaving her no chance to say no again, more vehemently.

And rousing her curiosity.

She shoved the ice cream back in the freezer, put on some fresh lipstick to meet the people she had no interest in meeting, then headed to her house one last time. Again.

Chapter Eighteen

Dixie didn't see any vehicles except Joe's truck when she reached the house. She parked out front, trying to mask her irritation that he'd made her come here. She would meet the new owners soon enough. She wanted time to get used to the idea first, not put faces to them.

She stalked up to the front door. Was she supposed to knock? Wouldn't the people think that was strange? *She* would.

She reached for the knob. The door opened.

"Hi," Joe said, giving her room to get past him.

She looked around. "Where is everyone?"

"I want you to keep an open mind, okay?"

What? Why? What could be wrong with them? She

couldn't voice her questions out loud, for fear of being overheard, but she craned her neck to look down the hallway, seeing nothing. No one.

"What's going on?" she whispered. "I don't see anyone. Where are the buyers?"

"They're here."

"Where? Are they in the garden?"

He took her hands. She tried to pull back.

"No. They're right here," he said, holding tighter.

"Here? You mean *us*?"

She'd never seen him like this, so strangely calm yet anxious. She didn't know what his game was, but she didn't want to be lured into bed again. She would resist him this time. She was well on the road to recovery over him and absolutely would not give in to him—or her own needs—again.

She couldn't let him think he could come home from a trip and find her available every time. His next trip would be for six months!

"I can't do this again, Joe." She pulled free and headed to the door, grabbed the handle. She could not sleep with him again. "I can't."

"Can't do what? Can't marry me?"

She stopped dead. "What?"

"This isn't how I planned it," he said, coming up beside her. "I know I blew the big romantic moment. Turn around, please."

She couldn't have heard him right. Marry him? How could that happen?

"Your hands are cold," he said, rubbing them between his. "I love you, Dixie. There's never been another girl—woman—for me. I can't stand the thought of being away from you ever again. I want to marry you, and have babies with you and live right here in Chance City, where we belong."

"You do?"

He nodded.

"But…"

"But what?"

She was totally confused. He was saying what she'd wanted to hear for such a long time, but it didn't make sense. "You told Kincaid to accept the offer."

"I rescinded it. I don't want to live anywhere else. We can add on or build another story. Do whatever we need to make it work for us. Because it's our house, Dix. We need it."

"But…what about your business?"

"I'll look for someone to join forces with me. We can share the load, each of us traveling less." His expression was earnest. "I've found I don't need as much change as I thought. Everyone told me to go and enjoy myself, to let go of all the responsibility I carry around. But I found it's not all it's cracked up to be. Some things are ingrained, you know? Without it I feel a little lost."

She was still confused. "What about this overseas job? What's that about?"

"How'd you hear about that?"

"We live in Chance City, Joe."

He smiled a little. "Yeah. Well, David lined it up for me."

"David Falcon?"

"He's been doing a lot of business in Tumari, which is a small, oil-rich country near Dubai, although not quite as extravagantly wealthy. The sultan wants to create eco-friendly landscaping, especially since they often have water shortage problems."

"That sounds like something you'd love to do."

He cupped her face. "You're something I'd love to do."

She laughed, a little breathlessly, her stress starting to dissipate as she was also starting to believe what he was saying.

"Your business is brand-new, Dixie," he said. "I wouldn't ask you to leave it. There'll be other opportunities for me closer to home."

"I want to go with you."

"What? No. You can't. You're just getting started."

It was her turn to hold on to him, to get him to see she was serious. "I want to see the world, too. With you. This would be our chance, before we start having children. I want you to take the job. I want to go with you. We could take short trips other places from there, right? See more of the world? And I could fly home every so often, check how everything is doing here. Maybe Shana would like to manage the salon. Maybe I'd need to find someone else. But this is a once-in-a-lifetime opportunity." She wrapped her arms around him. "I love you, too, Joey. I never stopped. Yes, I'll marry you. Take me to Tumari for a long honeymoon, please."

"I can't believe I'm so lucky," he said, cupping her face. "We wasted so much time."

"No, we didn't. We had to be apart to find each other again, because this time it'll be even stronger and more secure. We had to become separate in order to become a couple again. There's no one else for me." She kissed him then pulled back a little. "I only heard this morning that you were supposed to be leaving. What happened since then?"

"You happened." He brushed her hair with his hands. "I came to tell you about the deal, so that you wouldn't hear it from someone else. Then I saw you holding up that wedding dress in front of you, and the look on your face, and I knew it was what I wanted, too. Needed. It didn't matter anymore that I go places and do things. I just want to be with you. But thank you for figuring out a way for both of those things to happen."

"Home is where the heart is," she said.

"I was just thinking that. Now," he said, taking a step back, slipping his hand into his pocket and bringing out an engagement ring. He got onto one knee. "I love you with everything I have, everything I am, Dixie Callahan. I want to marry you and raise children together and watch their children grow."

She knelt, too. "It would be my honor."

He slid the ring on her finger and kissed it, then her lips.

Tomorrow they would gather the clan for a party, she

thought, but for tonight they would cherish what they'd rediscovered, and look to the future.

At long last, she would be his bride.

* * * * *

Kay Young returned to woozy consciousness to find that she was lying on a soft sofa beneath a heap of quilts near a cheerfully burning fire. When she tried to move, however, everything hurt, and she groaned.

At once she heard a sound, then a stranger with a hard, harsh face was squatting beside her. "Shh," he said softly. "You're safe here. I promise."

"I have to go," she said weakly, struggling against pain. "He'll find me. He can't find me."

"Easy, lady," he said quietly. "You're hurt. No one's going to find you here."

"He will," she said desperately, terror clutching at her insides. "He always finds me!"

"Easy," he said again. "There's a blizzard outside. No one's getting here tonight, not even the doctor. I know, because I tried."

"Doctor? I don't need a doctor! I've got to get away."

"There's nowhere to go tonight," he said levelly. "And if I thought you could stand, I'd take you to a window and show you."

But even as she tried once more to pull away the quilts, she remembered something else: this man had been gentle when he'd found her beside the road, even when she had kicked and clawed. He hadn't hurt her.

Terror receded just a bit. She looked at him and detected signs of true concern there.

The terror eased another notch and she let her head sag on the pillow. "He always finds me," she whispered.

"Not here. Not tonight. That much I can guarantee."

Will Kay's mysterious rescuer
protect her from her worst fears?
Find out in HER HERO IN HIDING
by New York Times *bestselling author Rachel Lee.*
Available June 2010,
only from Silhouette® Romantic Suspense.

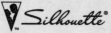

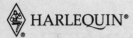

The Best Man in Texas
TANYA MICHAELS

Brooke Nichols—soon to be Brooke Baker—
hates surprises. Growing up in an unstable
environment, she's happy to be putting down
roots with her safe, steady fiancé. Then she meets
his best friend, Jake McBride, a firefighter and
former soldier who's raw, unpredictable and
passionate. With his spontaneous streak and
dangerous career, Jake is everything Brooke is
trying to avoid…so why is it so hard to resist him?

**Available June
wherever books are sold.**

"LOVE, HOME & HAPPINESS"

HARLEQUIN® *Romance*®

GIRLS' *Weekend in* VEGAS

Four friends, four dream weddings!

On a girly weekend in Las Vegas, best friends Alex, Molly, Serena and Jayne are supposed to just have fun and forget men, but they end up meeting their perfect matches! Will the love they find in Vegas stay in Vegas?

Find out in this sassy, fun and wildly romantic miniseries all about love and friendship!

Saving Cinderella! by MYRNA MACKENZIE
Available June

Vegas Pregnancy Surprise by SHIRLEY JUMP
Available July

Inconveniently Wed! by JACKIE BRAUN
Available August

Wedding Date with the Best Man
by MELISSA MCCLONE
Available September

www.eHarlequin.com

HRI7663

REQUEST YOUR FREE BOOKS!
2 FREE NOVELS PLUS 2 FREE GIFTS!

SPECIAL EDITION
Life, Love and Family!

YES! Please send me 2 FREE Silhouette® Special Edition® novels and my 2 FREE gifts (gifts are worth about $10). After receiving them, if I don't wish to receive any more books, I can return the shipping statement marked "cancel." If I don't cancel, I will receive 6 brand-new novels every month and be billed just $4.24 per book in the U.S. or $4.99 per book in Canada. That's a saving of 15% off the cover price! It's quite a bargain! Shipping and handling is just 50¢ per book.* I understand that accepting the 2 free books and gifts places me under no obligation to buy anything. I can always return a shipment and cancel at any time. Even if I never buy another book from Silhouette, the two free books and gifts are mine to keep forever.

235/335 SDN E5RG

Name _____ (PLEASE PRINT)

Address _____ Apt. #

City _____ State/Prov. _____ Zip/Postal Code

Signature (if under 18, a parent or guardian must sign)

Mail to the **Silhouette Reader Service:**
IN U.S.A.: P.O. Box 1867, Buffalo, NY 14240-1867
IN CANADA: P.O. Box 609, Fort Erie, Ontario L2A 5X3

Not valid for current subscribers to Silhouette Special Edition books.

Want to try two free books from another line?
Call 1-800-873-8635 or visit www.morefreebooks.com.

* Terms and prices subject to change without notice. Prices do not include applicable taxes. N.Y. residents add applicable sales tax. Canadian residents will be charged applicable provincial taxes and GST. Offer not valid in Quebec. This offer is limited to one order per household. All orders subject to approval. Credit or debit balances in a customer's account(s) may be offset by any other outstanding balance owed by or to the customer. Please allow 4 to 6 weeks for delivery. Offer available while quantities last.

Your Privacy: Silhouette is committed to protecting your privacy. Our Privacy Policy is available online at www.eHarlequin.com or upon request from the Reader Service. From time to time we make our lists of customers available to reputable third parties who may have a product or service of interest to you. If you would prefer we not share your name and address, please check here. ☐

Help us get it right—We strive for accurate, respectful and relevant communications. To clarify or modify your communication preferences, visit us at www.ReaderService.com/consumerschoice.

SSE10R